The Christmas Barn

The Christmas Barn
C.L. Davis

American Girl

Published by Pleasant Company Publications
Text Copyright © 2001 by C.L. Davis
Cover Illustration Copyright © 2001 by Raúl Colón
For information, address: Book Editor,
Pleasant Company Publications,
8400 Fairway Place, P.O. Box 620998,
Middleton, WI 53562.

Visit our Web site at **americangirl.com**

Printed in the United States of America.
First Edition
03 04 05 06 07 08 RRD 10 9 8 7 6 5 4 3

American Girl® is a registered trademark of Pleasant Company.

PICTURE CREDITS
The author has generously given permission to
reprint photographs contained in the end matter.

Cover Art by Raúl Colón

Library of Congress Cataloguing-in-Publication Data

Davis, C. L., 1959–
The Christmas barn / C.L. Davis.
p. cm.
Summary: In 1930, when a snowstorm destroys their home
in the Appalachian mountains, twelve-year-old Roxie and her family move
into the barn and prepare for a very unusual Christmas celebration.
ISBN 1-58485-414-6
[1. Family life–North Carolina–Fiction. 2. Snow–Fiction. 3. Christmas–Fiction.
4. North Carolina–Fiction.] I. Title.

PZ7.D28557 Ch 2001

[Fic]–dc21   2001031162

*For Scott and Abbe who encourage,
and for Mama who told me stories.*

Contents

1 · *Fetchin' Water*

I crouched close to the ground watchin' the woolly worm crawl over the planks that covered the well. It scrunched itself up and arched its back toward the sky, then stretched out so it could move a little further. It looked like an awful lot of work and made me glad that I had legs to help me get around. I took a deep breath and blew on it to help it go faster, but that only made it stop and stay where it was. I tried again, watchin' my breath as it fogged up in the cold air. This time, the worm curled up into a ball, makin' it look like a marble that had sprouted whiskers.

The door opened and Mama called out, "Roxie!"

I picked up a pine needle and poked at the woolly worm, but it pretended that I wasn't there. "Stupid worm, I'm just tryin' to help you. Don't pretend you can't hear me."

Mama called out again. "Roxie, can you hear me?"

"Yeah, Mama!"

"Are you filling that bucket, or did you fall in the well?"

"I'm gettin' it now, Mama!"

For as long as I can remember, fetchin' water was one of my chores and the one that I've always hated the most. I've lost count, but I'm sure that I'd carried at least a million buckets full by the time I reached my fifth year.

"Well, hurry up," shouted Mama. "I need to be startin' supper. Is Frank out there?"

"No, Mama, I think he's in the barn."

"Send him in. I need his help."

"I will!"

"And don't stay out there too long. You'll freeze!"

The door closed and I heard the latch fasten.

Mama always needed extra help from Frank when our Papa was gone. Frank was the oldest; then there were my sisters, Frankie and Inez. That put me fourth in peckin' order. After me was Ruby, and John was the baby. He was almost four years old then, but everybody still called him Baby John— at least everybody but me. I called him John. I'd always thought that it sounded funny and sometimes wondered if they would still call him Baby John after he was all grown up.

I picked up a maple leaf that was stuck between two of the planks and scooped up the woolly worm. I carried it over to the woodshed and put it on the ground. "You'll be safer here. If you get wet, you'll freeze up and stay a fuzzy ball of ice until the spring thaw." I went back to the well and reached for the pump handle. The rusty iron felt like ice in my hand. I began to pump, waitin' for the water to work its way out of the ground.

The summer had been long and hot, and Papa said that a bad summer would mean a bad winter. All the signs sure made it look that way. The mules' and cows' hair was thicker than usual. Tree bark was heaviest on the north side. Even the woolly worm had a heavy coat. Papa said it was nature's way of protectin' 'em, but he reckoned that us people had to rely on our good sense to survive the winter.

As the bucket filled and flowed over the top, I saw Frank walkin' up from the barn. He wore his heavy coat and a red knitted cap that hid most of his thick brown hair. Hair so thick that some people wondered how he ever got a comb through it. Frank was strong and tall, the spittin' image of my papa. There were about a dozen girls at our school, besides my sisters and me, and all of 'em were just crazy about Frank. One of 'em even wrote him a love letter. It said:

As sure as the rat runs across the rafter,
you're the boy that I am after.

Inez found the letter and read it out loud. Everybody laughed until tears ran down their faces. That is, everybody except for Frank. He just stood there with his face turnin' red. Almost as red as the cap he was wearin' now.

I called out to him. "Mama's lookin' for you!"

He walked toward me, brushing a bit of straw off of his coat sleeve. "What does she want?"

Whenever I saw a chance to get somebody else to fetch the water bucket, I jumped to it like lightnin'. "She wants you to bring her this water."

Frank started to speak, then stopped for a moment and brushed off another fleck of straw. "If she wants me to, then I reckon I'll have to do it."

He reached for the handle, then dipped his hand into the bucket, scooped it full of the icy water, and splashed it into my face. The cold water made me take in such a breath that I thought my lungs would burst. Frank flashed a grin. "Serves you right for tryin' to trick your big brother!"

He ran for the cabin with me right behind him, splashin' water on my legs as I ran.

"Wait till I get my hands on you, Frank Dockery!"

2 · *Waitin'*

I nez read out loud to us as Mama cooked supper. John interrupted, as he was known to do. "When will Papa get home?" he asked for the third time in ten minutes.

"He'll be here directly," Mama answered as she kneaded the bread dough. "He went to the church to pick up the mail."

Frankie picked up John and plopped him down into the rocker, tryin' to give Mama some peace. "Now don't ask Mama again," Frankie scolded. "She's tryin' to fix supper. Sit here and let Inez finish the story."

John was always excited when Papa went to get the mail, and so were the rest of us. We only got our mail once a month. The post office was in Murphy, and that was nearly twenty miles away. Since we couldn't always make the trip, a man named Andy Haas would bring the mail to the church on the third Saturday of each month. That was only five miles away.

Daddy Haas (that's what all of us kids called him) owned the rollin' store. It was a big wagon that was pulled by two brown mules. He sold things like cloth, pots, pans, and a few fancy things that nobody could really afford to waste their money on—things like hand lotion and chewing gum. We all thought the world of Daddy Haas. He was a tall man with a thick red beard, and he always had a big smile on his face. Most of the time he would be whistlin' a tune or tellin' a funny story. Mama always said that we were lucky to have Daddy Haas. That if it wasn't

for him, she'd feel like we were livin' on the moon.
If he didn't have what you needed in his wagon,
he'd bring it to you on his next trip. That was
important, 'cause people like us who lived in the
North Carolina mountains only went to a big
town like Murphy a few times a year.

Every fall, Mama and Papa would load our
wagon with jars of honey, sacks of seed corn, and
dried apples. They'd sell 'em to Mr. Shakelford,
the man who owned the store in Murphy. Then, just
as quick as they got the money, they'd turn around
and spend part of it on things that we couldn't
make or grow ourselves, like salt and kerosene.
One or two of us youngins always got to go with 'em
on that trip, but the rest of us had to stay home. In
the spring, Papa would go into town by himself, to
pay taxes. Nobody wanted to go on that trip, not
even Mama, 'cause Papa would cuss and say awful
things. Mama would stay at home and read from

the Bible, I reckon so as to even things out with the Lord. Then, a few days before Christmas, Mama and Papa would make another trip. That would be coming up real soon, 'cause today was December the eighteenth and the holiday was on its way.

I would start wishin' for Christmas as soon as we finished the Thanksgiving turkey, and I'd talk about it nonstop until it finally arrived. Mama would say, "Roxie, there's no use tryin' to rush Christmas. It'll get here when it gets here, and there's nothin' you can do to make it come any sooner." Deep down inside I knew that she was right, but it sure didn't make the waitin' any easier. After all, Christmas only came once a year, and it was the one day that I could always count on bein' special. There was always lots of good food and some presents. Mama and Papa would give each of us a few sticks of store-bought candy. If it was a real good year, maybe there would be a storybook for all of us to share or somethin' of that sort. Those things were nice, but most important, Christmas meant that Grandpa George and Grandma Vic would be comin' for a visit. They were always there on Christmas Night, fussin' over me, my brothers, and my sisters. Then, when I couldn't keep my eyes open for another minute, my Grandma Vic would always be there to say, "Night-night, my little Roxie." Havin' them in our house was what made Christmas special to me. They would be here in seven short days, and I could hardly wait.

"When will Papa get home?" John asked again.

Mama let out a sigh. "Frankie, would you take the baby up to the loft and keep him quiet?"

"Yes, Mama. Come on, Baby John." Frankie pulled John over to the ladder, and they headed up into the loft. That's where us youngins slept—Frank on one side and us girls on the other. Under the loft was a room for Mama and Papa. John slept there, too. Then there was the big room, where we cooked, ate, worked, and did everything that wasn't sleepin'. There was a long table with eight chairs around it. Two more chairs rested against the wall. They were for when we had company, but we didn't have company that often.

At one end of the room was Mama's cookstove. It was in the house when Papa bought the place, but he had to pay three dollars extra for it. The wall near the stove was lined with plank shelves, from the floor clear up to the rafters. The shelves were loaded with jars of canned goods, sacks of flour, plates, and tin cups. There was hardly an inch of the shelves that didn't have somethin' stacked on it. You could barely see the wall behind 'em.

At the other end of the room was a big stone fireplace. That's where Mama's rockin' chair sat. Our house wasn't like the houses I'd seen in town. They were made with cut boards and some of 'em were built with bricks. Our house was made out of thick logs that were cut down square, then stacked one on top of another, with mud in between each log. It was what they called a hand-hewn log house. All the houses up in the mountains were made like that. Papa didn't build our house. It had been there so long, we didn't even know who built it. But before us, a German man from Pennsylvania lived there. He built our barn and most of the outbuildings.

Mama put the bread dough on top of the woodstove to rise, then turned to me. "Roxie, I need another bucket of water."

Frank chuckled, and I gave him a burnin' look that could fry eggs.

"Ruby, you go to the springhouse and bring up the butter pail."

I got the water bucket. Ruby and I put on our coats, and we headed out the door.

3 · Panthers

When we were outside, Ruby said, "I'll get the water this time if you want me to and you can go to the springhouse." The springhouse was down near the creek, a good piece from the house.

"No, that's all right. I'm used to it." I kept walkin' and then realized that Ruby had stopped. I turned around.

"What's the matter?"

"It's gettin' dark. I don't wanna go by myself," Ruby whined, with her feet firmly planted.

"Why not, Ruby?"

"I'm skeered."

"Skeered of what?" I asked, but I already knew the answer.

"Panthers!" She looked down at the ground, embarrassed.

"You don't need to be skeered of panthers. Remember what Papa says—panthers are more skeered of people than people are of them."

I turned and started to walk away, but Ruby grabbed me by the back of my coat. "Mama's panther wasn't skeered!" As much as I hated to admit it, she was right. We'd both heard Mama and Papa tell the story hundreds of times.

Before I was born, when Frank and Frankie were just babies, my folks lived about forty miles from Murphy, near Teleco Plains, Tennessee. It was Mama and Papa's first house, a one room shack. Mama said it made the house we lived in now look like one of those fine houses in Murphy.

That November, Papa had butchered a hog. The weather was cold, and the meat wouldn't spoil before it could be salted down and stored until it was needed.

Papa decided that he'd take some of the fresh meat to the other side of the mountain to give to Grandpa George and Grandma Vic. He'd have to be gone overnight, since it was a far piece to travel. Mama and the babies would have to be left alone. Papa asked Mama if she'd be all right by herself without her "big strong man there to protect her."

"Course I will, Bass," Mama said. "Now get out of here so I can get back to my work."

Mama sent Papa on his way. She had to stay home and work at gettin' the hog ready for the smokehouse and grindin' up parts to make sausage and such. Nothin' was left to waste. Even the hog's guts were used to make soap. Soap you used to wash your clothes, your dishes, and yourself, too.

Mama put the hog guts on the roof of the cabin to keep the dogs away from 'em until it was time to make the soap. Then she went inside.

A bit after nightfall, she heard what she thought was a woman screamin'. She ran out onto the porch to see who it might be. She came face-to-face with a big panther that must have been at least seven feet long. She froze in her tracks with the panther lookin' her straight in the eyes. Then the panther let out another scream, and that sent Mama into the house in one leap. She pulled down the board that locked the door and got the gun. It was an old cap'n ball rifle that my great-grandpapa had used in the Civil War. She loaded it, but it took a while 'cause her hands were shakin' so. She sat on the bed with Frank on one side, Frankie on the other, and waited.

After a few minutes, she heard the panther leap up onto the roof. The shack wasn't that sturdy to begin with, and she was afraid that the big cat might claw its way through and kill all of 'em. Mama got up off the bed, listened for the spot on the rooftop where the panther was clawing, raised the gun, and bang!

The next day, Papa got back in the late afternoon. Mama was out in the yard boilin' the hog guts and lye to make soap. Papa ran over, picked Mama up, and gave her a big hug.

"Did you miss me, my helpless woman? Did you get on fine without your big strong man here to protect ya?"

Mama said, "Put me down. There's no time for that. We've got work to do! I've gotta finish makin' the soap, and you've gotta fix that hole in the roof before it rains!"

Papa looked at her and said, "What hole? I don't remember there bein' a hole up there."

"Well, climb up that ladder and see for yourself."

Just when Papa reached the top rung of the ladder, he saw the panther layin' there on its belly.

He didn't know it was dead. He let out a yelp, fell off the ladder, and hit the ground with a thud.

Mama walked over to where he had landed and looked down at him. "While you're up there, 'my big strong man,' why don't you drag down that old panther I shot? I'd do it myself, but I'm just a helpless woman."

Papa loved to tell that story, and whenever he told it, he'd always say, "After that I've never worried about leavin' Callie Dockery on her own again, but I do pity anything, man or beast, that might get in her way."

4 · *A Skeerdy-Cat and a Stubborn Mule*

R uby, that's just one of Mama's stories! Mama tells us lots of stories," I said as I turned to walk away.

I didn't go more than a couple steps before Ruby yelled out, "It ain't just a story, it's a true story! Now, are you gonna go with me or not?"

I kept walkin' as I said, "Not." The next thing I knew, Ruby jumped on my back and almost knocked me to the ground. She started beggin' into my ear, "Please, Roxie, please!"

"All right, I'll go with you," I said as I yanked her arms from around my neck. "Then you can help me get the water. But you'll have to do the pumpin' and carry the bucket, too." She smiled and said, "OK, Roxie." Then she skipped toward the springhouse, leavin' me standin' there with the water bucket still in my hand.

Ruby was two years younger than me but almost as big. She had thick blond hair that framed her round face and bright blue eyes that danced and sparkled when she laughed. She had a sprinkle of freckles across her nose. Not too many, just enough to make it interstin'.

Most people said that we looked almost alike, and I reckon it was so. 'Cept Ruby had straight hair and mine had a bit of a curl.

One time when I was almost eight years old, Ruby and me were playin' in the churchyard after Sunday service. A woman that we'd never seen before came up and started talkin' to Mama. She said that she thought Ruby and me were two of the prettiest youngins that she'd ever seen. Mama looked at us and said, "Y'all go over there and play. I'll be along directly."

We walked away and sat on a tree stump. Ruby and me stayed real quiet, and both of us looked down at the ground, tryin' to pretend that we weren't listenin'. That woman kept talkin' a mile a minute, and when she said, "Why, that one ought to be in the movie pictures," Ruby and me looked up quick as two whips, but she had already dropped her pointin' finger.

After we left the church and headed for home, Ruby caught up with me and asked, "Who do you reckon that woman was talkin' about?" I picked up my speed and left her behind as I answered, "I reckon she was talkin' about me." Ruby huffed at me and hardly talked to me for the rest of the week.

I reckon it was kind of hateful of me to get her riled up that way, but I have to admit that it was awful fun. And it worked every time. Whenever we'd get into a fuss, I used to say, "That woman at the church said that I was the prettiest."

Course, it would make Mama madder than it did Ruby. Mama would say, "That woman said nothin' of the sort and you ought not say such things, Roxie! You ain't got need to be so vain!"

After that I'd just whisper it to Ruby every now and then. But I'd pretend I didn't say a thing when she'd run to tell Mama. Though I reckon Mama knew. Mama always seemed to know what was and what wasn't.

When we got to the springhouse, Ruby looked over her shoulder. "Now don't leave till I come out."

"Don't worry. I won't."

She started to open the door, then stopped. "What if there's a panther in there, or a bear?"

"Don't be such a skeerdy-cat. Just go in and get the butter."

"But it'll be dark in there! Go get it for me, Roxie, pleeeease."

I rolled my eyes, let out a groan, and did it myself just to get the whole thing over with. As I opened the door, Ruby added, "Just don't tell Mama."

The springhouse was a small shed that was partly in the ground and partly above. The half that was buried was made out of rock. So was the floor. The top part was wood. There were six log steps that led down to the door. When that door opened, there was another door. It was like a shed inside of a shed. Water from an underground spring flowed through a pipe that stuck out of one of the walls. The water passed through and drained out the other side, makin' its way down to the creek.

The water was always the same, summer and winter. It was icy cold but would never freeze. We kept our butter, milk, cheese, and things like that in the springhouse. They wouldn't spoil so quick in there. And dogs and other animals couldn't get to 'em, not even panthers or bears.

I came out of the springhouse, closin' both doors behind me. Ruby came up to me, took the butter pail out of my hand, then kissed me on the cheek. "Thank you, Roxie. You're a good sister."

I just hated it when she did things like that. Sometimes I believe she did 'em just to take the fun out of our fightin'.

Just as we finished fillin' the water bucket, I saw Papa comin' up the road. Well, we called it a road, but it wasn't much more than a path, just wide enough for a wagon to get through. Years ago, it was a trail that was used by the Cherokee. Grandpa George told me so, and he'd know, 'cause his mama was one of 'em. When I told people I had Cherokee blood in me, they thought I was fibbin', what with my blond hair and blue eyes, but I knew that it was true. Grandpa wouldn't lie.

Papa had a sack thrown over his shoulder and was walkin' at a good clip. He never took the wagon if he was only goin' five miles or so. He'd say, "No point in wearin' out the mules if we're only goin' that far." I always thought it was odd that we had to walk five miles to school and five miles back, while the mules rested in the barn, munchin' on feed corn. I sometimes envied those mules.

"Papa's home!" Ruby hollered when she spotted him. She dropped the butter pail on the ground and ran down the road to meet him.

"Wait, Ruby, don't forget the butter!"

When she reached him, she leaped up into the air, throwin' her arms around his neck and her legs around his waist. He caught her with his free arm and spun around twice as she hugged him.

The door opened and Mama called out, "Roxie, where's that water?"

"I'm comin', Mama! Papa's home! Ruby ran

down to meet him. But she forgot to get the . . ."

"Well, hurry up then. I don't wanna stand here talkin' all night. I'm lettin' out all the heat." She went back inside, closin' the door behind her.

I let out a groan as I picked up the water bucket and the butter pail and headed for the house. I stopped to look back at Papa. Ruby was still wrapped around him, gettin' a free ride to the warmth of the house. As I stood there watchin' 'em pass by, it made me think of those mules again, all safe and cozy in the barn. Then I made up my mind that I wasn't gonna budge an inch until things got evened out somehow. I put down the buckets, crossed my arms, and shouted, "I sure do wish those mules would tell me their secret to an easier life!"

Papa stopped at the door, turned around, and said, "Now stop your fussin', Roxie girl. Let's get on inside."

I didn't give him a response. I just stood there

with my feet firmly planted. He plopped Ruby down onto the porch. "There ain't no need to be so stubborn, Roxie girl. Now, are you comin' into the house, or are you thinkin' about movin' into the barn with the mules? You ought to get along fine with them—you're every bit as stubborn as they are!"

Ruby let out a big laugh and disappeared into the house. I picked up the buckets as Papa walked back down the path. He reached for the heavy water bucket. "Let me carry that for you, Roxie. You look all tired out."

"Thank you, Papa," I said as I released the handle.

"You work too hard, Roxie. You ought to take time to rest every once in a while. You look like you're about to fall asleep on your feet."

"Sometimes I think that I might," I said as we headed toward the doorway.

Papa stopped and said, "Maybe this'll wake you up." He dipped his fingers into the bucket, flung a bit of cold water in my face, and ran into the house. He let out a laugh and yelled, "Help me, Callie, Roxie's after me!"

I ran right behind him, laughin' and shoutin', "Papa, you're as bad as Frank! Now I know where he gets it from!"

5 · The Mail

By the time we started supper, I'd forgiven Ruby. That was always the way. I'd get mad at her, but I couldn't stay mad long. After all, she was my little sister, and as much as I hated to admit it, I loved her.

Supper was good that night, but everything Mama made was good. Papa used to say that he only married Mama for her cookin'. Mama would shoot him a look. Then he'd say somethin' like, ". . . well, her cookin' and her housekeepin', her cookin' and her sewin', her cookin' and that sweet face of hers." By that time, Mama would always and we only saw her about once a year.

"Well, open it up so we can hear what she has to say," Papa said as he put the sack on the table beside him.

Inez carefully tore open the envelope and pulled out what was inside. "It's a Christmas card." She held it up for all of us to see. On the front was a picture of a pine tree with snow on it. Except the snow wasn't painted on. It was glued there and looked like the real thing. It sparkled in the light of the fire. Inez opened the card and read what was written inside:

Wishing you the happiest of times
during this Christmas season.
All my love,
Tiny

Inez closed the card. "The first part was printed in the card, but Aunt Tiny wrote the 'All my love' part."

Papa took the card. "It's real nice to hear from Tiny."

blush and smile. I'd always smile, too.

We always talked when we had supper time, sometimes eight conversations at once. But tonight, Papa had control of the conversation. When it was time to pick up the mail, he saw people that we didn't see for the rest of the month. Like the ones who didn't wanna go to church on Sunday or those who lived too far up in the mountains to make it regularly. Papa was filled up with the news that night. He sat there tellin' us who'd been sick, who's gettin' married, and those sorts of things. Then he said, "Daddy was there." That's what my papa called his papa, our Grandpa George. "And he's lookin' forward to comin' over for Christmas." I felt a tingle shoot up my spine as soon as those words came out of his mouth, and I started tappin' my shoes up and down on the floorboards.

Mama asked, "What's that racket?"

I grabbed my knees so I could stop my legs from

jumpin' up and down and said, "Nothin', Mama."

Then Papa gave us the news from Murphy. "Andy Haas says we're suppose to be in for a snow-storm. Says they expect it to be a bad one. Might start anytime now." We hadn't had any snow yet, and the news got us youngins excited. We always looked forward to the first snowfall. "I was lookin' at the sky when I came back from the church, and I think he might be right."

After supper, Papa sent Frank and Frankie out to get some firewood. Inez usually washed the dishes and I dried 'em, but tonight Mama said, "Ruby, you'll dry the dishes, since you were too afraid to go to the springhouse and made Roxie do it for you."

Ruby quickly jumped in. "You told!"

Mama handed her a dishrag. "Roxie didn't say nary a word. Now get to work." It's like I said, Mama always knew what was and what wasn't.

When the dishes were washed and the fire was blazin', Papa brought out the sack of mail. We all gathered around him to see what might have come. Lots of times there was no mail at all, for months and months. But this time we could see that sack was holdin' quite a load. First, Papa pulled out a letter. He handed it over to Inez. It wasn't for her, but she loved to read. She never had much to say on her own, but if it was somebody else's words, she loved to read 'em out loud. Mama used to say, "Inez could read the words right off the page, so there's nothin' left but plain white paper." Besides, Papa couldn't read anyhow. He only went to school for a few weeks in his whole life. Then he had to go to work to help his family.

Inez looked at the front of the letter. "It's from Aunt Tiny." Aunt Tiny was one of Mama's sisters. They called her that 'cause she was so small. She was a grown woman but not much bigger than me and Ruby. She lived sixty miles away in Tennessee,

Mama took the card from Papa. "I think it'll look pretty up here on the fire board."

We all looked up at the card for a moment, until John interrupted, as he was known to do. "What else is in the sack?"

Papa pulled out another letter and gave it to Inez. She was sittin' on the floor in front of Mama's rocker. Mama looked down at the envelope and let out a gasp. Then she flopped back down in her rocker. The light from the fire reflected in the tears wellin' up in her eyes.

Frankie stood up. "What's the matter, Mama?"

Inez looked at Frankie. "It's from Aunt Floss."

6 · *Aunt Floss*

Aunt Floss was another of Mama's sisters. She had left the mountains six years ago, and nobody had heard from her since. Some people said they thought she must have died. Now it was apparent that she was very much alive. I was glad to hear it, 'cause she was my favorite aunt, even though I hadn't seen her since I was six years old.

Frankie sat down on the floor. "Open it up."

As Inez tore open the envelope, none of us made a sound, not even John, as he wasn't known to do. Mama leaned over Inez's shoulder, readin' along with her, as Inez read the letter out loud.

Dear Callie,

I hope this letter finds you well and fine. I know I ought to have written you before now, but time just seems to get away from us. James and I have settled near the town of Chillicothe, in Ohio. It's a good size town with a lot of people. Bigger than Murphy, and a far cry from the mountain where we were raised. James bought a small farmhouse with a little plot of land. It's not much, but big enough to plant a garden, and there are a few fruit trees. The house needed a lot of work, but it was all that we could afford. James paid cash for it. We consider ourselves lucky that we found it and were able to get it before the Depression hit.

James gets some work now and then with a man who builds houses, but there ain't a whole lot of houses being built these days. I've been working in a store that sells dresses and hats and such. There are enough families here that haven't been wiped out by the Depression to keep the store going. James didn't want me to take the job, but I sat him down and gave him a good talking to. I told him that his pride was going to make us starve to death. Finally, he saw that it was the right thing to do. People have to take anything they can get in these hard times.

James says to tell Bass that he can't wait to come back for a visit so they can swap lies and trade nickels. Tell all the youngins that I send my love.

I'll be sending a package next week. It ought to reach you before Christmas. It's something that I thought would be perfect for . . ."

Mama snatched the letter out of Inez's hands. "Here, let me finish that. 'It's somethin' that I thought would be perfect for . . . makin' quilts.'

It's quiltin' scraps . . ."

Inez looked at Mama. "But Mama, that ain't what it . . ."

Mama cut her off. "Don't interrupt me while I'm readin'. Do you understand, Inez?"

"Oh . . . yeah, Mama, sorry."

Mama continued readin':

> *I hope your Christmas will be a good one, and that you will all have a happy 1931. I will write to you again soon.*
>
> *Your loving sister,*
>
> *Floss*

Mama folded the letter and held it close to her heart. Papa was lookin' at Mama with a little smile on his face. "I'm glad to hear that she's all right, Callie."

"So am I, Bass, so am I."

We all sat there silent for a moment, until John blurted out, "What's the Depression?"

Papa reached for John and pulled him up onto

his lap. "It's depressin', that's what it is, Baby John. It means that lots of folks are havin' hard times. But it's too complicated for you to understand. I ain't sure that I completely understand it myself."

I didn't understand it neither. But then again, I hardly even noticed it. We never had money to begin with. There was still food for the table and wood for the fire. Poor before the Depression was just the same as poor durin' the Depression.

John slid down off Papa's knee. "What else is in the sack?"

"Well now, let's see." Papa pulled out a box wrapped in brown paper. "There's a package. I reckon it must be the one from Aunt Floss."

Mama reached for it. "I'll take that. It'd be the quiltin' scraps."

Ruby chimed in, "Why would she send you quiltin' scraps?"

" 'Cause she wanted to."

"Ain't you gonna open it, Mama?"

Mama didn't give an answer as she took the package into her room. Through the doorway, I could see that she was puttin' the package in her big wooden trunk. Then she sat down on the bed and read the letter from Aunt Floss over and over.

Mama's trunk was a big pine box that her papa made for her when she was a girl. It's what they called a "hope chest." It was for collectin' things that you'd need when you got married, like pots and pans and blankets. But now, Mama kept her secret things in there. We were never allowed to look inside of the trunk, not even Papa. It was her only privacy. Sometimes she would show us things that were in the trunk, like locks of our hair from when we were babies and the ribbon that she wore in her hair when she and Papa got married. I didn't know much else about what was in it. Except now, I reckoned she kept quiltin' scraps in there.

Papa reached for the sack. "There's one more thing in this here bag." He reached in and pulled out the last piece of mail. As I looked at it, little shivers of excitement ran up and down my back.

7 · *The Book of Dreams*

Once a year somethin' truly magical happened. Somethin' that provided us with hour after hour of delightful entertainment. It was the arrival of the Sears & Roebuck catalogue.

Papa handed the thick paperback book to Inez. She laid it carefully down on the floor, as if it were a priceless treasure. Frankie brought the kerosene lamp from the table and placed it beside the catalogue. Then she turned up the wick so as to cast as much light on the pages as possible. I joined my brothers and sisters, each of us fightin' for every inch of space so we could get the best possible view. Inez turned to the first page and began to read, describin' each of the wonderful items as we looked at the pictures.

Buyin' things was just somethin' we dreamed about, and pretendin' with Sears & Roebuck was the closest thing that we had to makin' those dreams come true. Even Christmas didn't bring splendid things like what we saw in the catalogue. About the only things we got from the store were our shoes and some of our coats. Mama and Frankie made all of our clothes. They even knitted the stockins we wore. Shirts and dresses were made out of whatever they could find. John used to have a shirt that was made out of six old bandannas, each a different color. Mama used to say it was like the coat of many colors that Joseph in the Bible wore.

I'd only had one store-bought dress in my whole life. Aunt Floss bought that for me just before she went away. It was a blue print with long sleeves. It had lace around the cuffs and collar. I loved that dress and wore it every chance I got, not just for Sunday. Mama would fuss at me and say, "You're gonna wear that dress out." That was my intention, but I never told her so. When we outgrew our clothes, they would be handed down to the younger ones. I just couldn't stand the thought of Ruby wearin' my store-bought dress.

I never did completely wear it out, but I wore it until the lace cuffs were halfway up to my elbows and there wasn't any more hem to let out. As luck would have it, Ruby grew faster than I did and was nearly as big as me. So she never did get my dress. Mama finally cut it up, since there were no girls younger than Ruby. She sewed a big patch of it into a quilt. I never did know what happened to the rest of it. I supposed that she had used it for a cleanin' rag.

Each of us found somethin' of special interest to

us in the catalogue. I liked a bank I saw. It was a clown made out of cast iron. When you put a penny in its hand and pulled a lever, it would raise its arm and pop the coin into its mouth. Ruby spoiled it for me, though, by sayin', "I wouldn't want that. You wouldn't have any pennies for it to eat in the first place."

I told her that I'd use pebbles or twigs instead. But she said that it wouldn't be the same.

After about an hour, Mama came back into the room. "It's time for you youngins to get ready for bed."

We begged to stay up a little bit longer, so she gave us ten more minutes with Sears & Roebuck, while Frank and Frankie went out for more firewood. "Be sure to get some of the big hickory logs," Papa told 'em as they went out the door. "They'll burn through the night. And get one for in the mornin'."

Inez pointed to a picture of a tall clock in the

catalogue. "Look at this, Mama. Wouldn't you just love to have one of those?"

"I reckon it'd be nice."

Inez turned to the next page. "If I had a bunch of money, I could sure spend a lot of it in a hurry."

"A bunch of money would just make you miserable, Inez." None of us thought that was true, but we didn't say so to Mama.

She sat down in her rocker, and John climbed up into her lap. "When I get big and have some money, I'm gonna buy you somethin' from Sears & Roebuck."

Inez asked him, "What are you gonna buy her, Baby John?"

"I ain't sure yet. I'm torn between the washtub and a stick pony."

That made all of us burst out laughin', even Papa. "I can just picture your Mama prancin' 'round the house on a stick pony!"

John got mad and pouted, but Mama smoothed his ruffled feathers. "I think I'd be partial to the stick pony, Baby John. I already have a good washtub."

John looked at us. "See, I told you so."

The door opened, and Frank and Frankie came in with the big hickory logs under their arms. Frank shook his head hard, causin' big white flakes of snow to fall to the floor. "The snow's started! It's comin' down hard. The ground's already covered."

It had been a good Saturday. Sears & Roebuck, Aunt Floss, and the first snowfall, all in the same day.

8 · *Biscuits and Mama*

I was the first youngin to wake up the next mornin'. The sun hadn't come up yet, but the light from the kerosene lamp slipped up over the edge of the sleepin' loft. I pulled on my clothes, tryin' not to wake the others. On Sundays, I liked to be the first one up so I could spend a little quiet time with Mama. She was always up early to start the fire in the stove and make the biscuits. I climbed down the ladder without making a peep.

"Mornin', Mama," I said in a low voice.

"You skeered me, Roxie. I didn't hear you comin'."

"I didn't wanna wake the others."

She put a handful of small sticks in the firebox of the stove, then crossed to the fireplace for a shovelful of hot coals. She dumped the coals on the sticks and sprinkled some wood chips over 'em. After a bit, they flamed up, cracklin' and poppin' as they caught fire. Finally, she placed three nice pieces of split wood on the top and blew on 'em hard. That set 'em to blazin'. She closed the door and wiped her hands on the rag that was stuck in her apron. She got out the makins to fix the biscuits. The flour, the lard, the dough board, and such.

I stood by the ladder, watchin', thinkin' about things Papa would say about her, like ". . . I only married her for her cookin' and that sweet face of hers."

He was right. It was a sweet face.

Her hair was long, nearly down to her waist, but she wore it in a big bun put up on the back of her head. Her eyes were brown. I got my blue eyes from Papa, the Irish and Cherokee side of the family. Don't ask me how, but that's the way it happened. When Mama laughed, her eyes danced and sparkled. I got that part of my eyes from her.

I stayed quiet while she worked. I didn't wanna interrupt. Mama didn't like for us to bother her when she was cookin'. Then she said without lookin' around, "Do you wanna learn?"

"What?"

She turned to look at me. "I said, do you wanna learn? To make biscuits?"

I nodded yes. Frankie was the only one that she had taught how to make biscuits. She'd tried with Inez, but they always turned out hard and funny lookin'. Finally, Papa said that Inez wasn't allowed to make 'em anymore or we'd all waste away to nothin'. Inez didn't care—she didn't like to make 'em anyhow.

"Well, come over here and let me get you started."

I moved to the table and stood behind the bread bowl. Mama went behind me and began my lesson. "Now, this is the starter dough. It's what was left over from last night. You're gonna add to this." She sifted some flour into the bowl, her arms reachin' around on each side of me. Then she took hold of my hands with hers. Mama's hands were rough and calloused from all the hard work she did. She dipped my hand into the lard bucket. "You'll need at least this much, but you may need to add more later. Now you put in some water, a pinch of salt, a little bakin' powder, and you work the dough." We squished the mixture with our four hands, hers rubbin' against mine.

The lard made her hands feel soft, like she'd never worked a hard day in her life. "Now we put the dough on the dough board and sprinkle it with more flour. That'll keep it from stickin'." She gave me the rollin' pin and curled her fingers around mine. "You've watched Mama do this part, right?" I didn't answer. I was too busy concentratin' on the dough and lookin' at Mama's fingers. She began to guide my arms as we rolled out the dough. First this way, then that, foldin' it over, then rollin' it out again. "That's right, you're doin' real good." It felt like my arms were part of hers as we worked the dough, and I reckoned they were. She was my mama, and her blood was runnin' through my veins.

"There, that ought to just about do it." She handed me a tin cup. "Now cut 'em out with this. I'll grease the pans while you do." I cut out the perfect circles, twenty-four in all. That's how many biscuits Mama made every mornin'. We put 'em in two iron skillets and sat 'em on top of the stove.

"How do they look, Mama?"

She dipped her rag in the bucket of water

and rung it out. "They look good enough to eat . . . I hope." She laughed at her joke and so did I. Her eyes danced and sparkled, and I was sure that mine did, too. She took the damp rag and wiped the flour off of my hands, cleanin' each finger, takin' more time than it should've. I was glad. At that moment, I never wanted Mama to let go of my hands.

9 · *Snow*

A bit of daylight was comin' through the little window by Mama's rocker. The others would be wakin' up soon, and the house would be full of noises once again—noises like Inez readin' out loud, Ruby sayin' things to pester me, and John askin' questions and talkin' just to hear himself talk. But I'd had my quiet time with Mama, and it would last me for the rest of the week.

Mama took a half-gallon jar of canned black-berries off the shelf and emptied it into a big brown bowl. "Roxie, I need you to run down and get me some water."

"Yes, Mama." I slipped into my heavy brown coat and started for the door, swingin' the bucket as I walked. I lifted the latch and pulled the door open. Then I stopped dead in my tracks. "Mama!"

"What is it, Roxie?" Mama looked up and saw what I was hollerin' about. "Well, goodness to heavens!" she shouted as she looked at the doorway.

I'd forgotten all about the snow. I reckoned Mama had, too, but there was no forgettin' about it now. The porch was filled with snow, from top to bottom. A gnat couldn't have gotten through.

"Bass! Bass, wake up!"

Papa sprang into the room like a jackrabbit, still wearin' his long johns and lookin' confused. "What is it, Callie?"

Frank shimmied down the ladder, followed by the others. "What's the matter, Mama?"

She pointed to the doorway. "That's what's the matter!"

Papa dropped his jaw. "Great day in the mornin'!" He rushed to the little window, wiped the frost off the glass, and peered out. "At least we ain't buried alive. We can still get out of the window. Get dressed, youngins. There'll be no restin' this Sunday. We got work to do."

While the others got into their clothes, Mama finished gettin' breakfast ready. We sat down to eat before we started diggin' the house out. In all the excitement, Mama forgot to tell 'em that I had made the biscuits. That suited me just fine, 'cause knowin' Frank, he would've probably made fun of 'em anyhow. Instead, he sopped up the blackberry juice and crammed the bread into his mouth. It was my little secret, and it made me feel good inside.

After we finished, it was time to get to work. Papa opened the window and looked out. "Well, youngins, let's get to it."

Frank climbed out the window, then Frankie and

Inez. Papa picked Ruby up, put her through the window, then did the same with me. John wanted to go out, too, but Mama made him sit in her rocker and keep quiet.

As I lowered myself out the window, I sank into the snow. It came up nearly to my waist. We stood there lookin' around for a moment. Everything was white except for the gray sky. The big tall pine tree was heavy with snow. It leaned toward the house, its branches hangin' low, pointin' down toward the ground. Ruby tugged at Inez's coat sleeve. "It looks just like Aunt Tiny's Christmas card, don't it?"

Inez nodded in agreement. "It sure is pretty."

Frank sighed, "You won't think it's pretty after you've been diggin' for a while."

Papa handed us buckets and pans out of the window. "Start diggin'. Make a path to the door and I'll join you." He was too big to fit through the window, so it was up to us to clear the way.

We started scoopin' up the fluffy snow, throwin' it off to the side, workin' our way around the house and up onto the porch. In about a half an hour, we were almost there. As Frank scooped his bucket full, it scraped against the door and we could see a patch of brown wood. The door opened, and John popped his head through the hole in the snow. He smiled and said, "Hey, Frank."

After a few more minutes, we were back in the house. Mama grabbed the broom and swept up the snow that had fallen onto the floor, while we warmed ourselves by the fire. Then we were off to clear away more of the snow. Gettin' out the door was just the beginnin'. We had to make our way down to the barn, the outhouse, the chicken coop, the woodshed, and the smokehouse. All we could see of the springhouse was a little bit of the roof. The water pump was covered completely. I told Papa that I thought we should leave it that way; then I wouldn't have to carry water to the house. We could just melt snow instead. He didn't agree at all but looked at me and said, "Dig." And dig we did. It took us until dark, but we cleared paths to all the outbuildins.

That night at supper, we didn't talk like we usually did. Well, except for John. But he'd talk to a tree stump if there were no people around. The rest of us were just too tired. We didn't even have enough energy to look at the Sears & Roebuck catalogue. After the dishes were washed and the fire had been taken care of, Mama had Inez read a few verses to us from the Bible, since we hadn't made it to church that day.

After Inez finished, Mama said, "It's bedtime. You youngins have school tomorrow."

Papa looked up. "No, they don't. There are drifts of snow out there eight feet deep."

Mama argued with him. "Now, Bass, they need to go to school."

But he'd have none of it. "One of 'em's liable to fall in a hole and get killed. I wouldn't walk those five miles myself." Mama hadn't thought about that. Neither had we.

No school was a disappointment to us. We only went four months out of the year, November through February. The rest of the time we were needed at home to work. School was a heap easier. It was practically a holiday.

After Mama thought about it, she gave in. "I reckon you're right. Y'all can take your lessons here at home till some of the snow clears."

Mama picked up John and carted him off to bed. We climbed up the ladder to get ourselves ready, too. I crawled under the covers of the bed that I shared with Ruby. It felt good to lay there. My arms and back ached from all the diggin' I had done. Papa turned down the lamp and I could hear him puttin' another log on the fire. Then his heavy boots made their way over to the little window.

After a bit, Mama said in a low voice, "Bass, ain't you comin' to bed?"

Papa was quiet for a moment. Then he said, "It's snowin' again."

10 · *Disappointments*

The next mornin', none of us woke up till Mama called us down for breakfast. Papa sat at the table drinkin' his coffee, 'cept it wasn't real coffee. Mama would parch acorns and grind 'em up in the coffee mill, then brew 'em. It made a red coffee, but Papa said it tasted like the real thing.

"Mornin', Mama."

"Mornin', Roxie."

"Mornin', Papa." He didn't answer me. He just sat there sippin' his coffee, with a disgusted look on his face.

Frankie climbed down the ladder next. "Mornin', Mama."

"Mornin', Frankie."

"Mornin', Papa." He gave her the same response he'd given me.

Then John, who was sittin' in the rocker, explained, "Papa's mad 'cause it snowed more last night."

Frankie went to the window and looked out. "For goodness sake, it covered up all the diggin' we did yesterday!"

Papa put his cup down. "I hope y'all got a good night's sleep, 'cause we got more snow to shovel. Sorry, girls."

The thought of diggin' out all those paths again made me wanna climb back up into the sleepin' loft and hide under the covers. But, as Mama always said, "You've gotta do what's gotta be done and there's nothin' to be done but do it."

We had our breakfast and went to work. It wasn't as bad as the day before. At least this time we could get out of the house without havin' to climb through the window. But still, it was plenty bad enough. We got everything dug out by mid-afternoon. Then there were our regular chores to attend to.

The snow was still fallin', but just little flakes now. I was in the barn milkin' one of the cows. Inez was milkin' the other one. Frank and Frankie were feedin' and tendin' to the mules, and Ruby had just finished feedin' the chickens.

She came into the stall where we were workin'. "Look, I found two eggs! That ought to cheer Papa up." Chickens don't usually lay eggs in the wintertime.

Inez looked up from her milkin'. "That's good, Ruby. Be careful you don't break 'em."

Ruby huffed and said, "I won't."

I watched the milk as it squirted into my bucket.

It reminded me of the snow we'd been diggin'.
"I hate white. It's my least favorite color."

Frank was in the next stall. Since he was the oldest, he seemed to think that he knew everything. He was always correctin' the rest of us. "White ain't a color. White's . . . well, it's just white. It's like . . . nothin'."

I was always ready to bicker with Frank. "White is so a color, ain't it, Frankie?" She was in the other stall. She didn't answer. "Ain't it, Frankie?"

"Yes, it's a color! Now I wish the two of you would stop fussin'!"

I continued my work, tryin' to think about any color except white. I fixed a color in my mind and concentrated on it. "I think blue's my favorite color. Do you like blue, Frank? . . . Frank, do you like blue?"

"Yeah, yeah, yeah, I like blue."

"Frankie, that dress we were lookin' at in the

catalogue, do you think you could make one?"

She came into the stall. "I could make just about any dress in that book."

"And would it be blue, a blue print, with lace around the cuffs and collar?"

"It would be if I had some blue print cloth and some lace."

Frank came into the stall carrying the pitchfork he'd been workin' with. "Maybe you could get some old white cloth and dye it with some blueberry juice."

I stopped my milkin'. "Then it'd be just blue, Frank. Just blue ain't a blue print." He shoved his pitchfork into the ground.

Ruby sat down on the straw next to my milk stool. "Who knows, Roxie, maybe Papa will get you some blue print cloth when he goes into town to get our Christmas candy." Inez stopped her work, and none of us said a word for a moment. Ruby looked at each of us. "What did I do?"

Frankie took her by the hand and pulled her up. "Nothin', Ruby. I'm all done here. Let's take the eggs inside and show 'em to Mama."

The three of us waited until they left the barn before we spoke. None of us had thought about Papa not bein' able to get into town. But it looked like the snow would make it impossible. I stood up and said, "It's five more days till Christmas. Maybe the snow will melt before then, right?"

Inez answered me by sayin' nothin' and goin' back to her milkin'. Frank took the pitchfork handle and swayed it back and forth. Then he picked up a piece of straw and stuck one end of it into his mouth. After a moment, he brought up somethin' else. "I reckon Grandpa and Grandma won't make it for Christmas this year. They're nearly seventy. They'll never be able to make it across the mountain."

We finished our work in the barn and headed

back to the house. When we got outside, we saw that the snow had turned to sleet. It bounced off our coats like tiny pebbles as we walked along.

As we neared the porch, I looked up at the big tall pine tree. Its branches were trimmed with ribbons of snow, and it sparkled against the pale gray sky. That put somethin' else in my mind, yet another disappointment.

11 · *Pesterin'*

Two nights before Christmas, people from miles around would meet at the church. There'd be a church service and then the tree decoratin'. People in the mountains didn't put Christmas trees up in their houses. We all shared the one at the church.

People would bring food and put it on a big table for everybody to share. After the tree was decorated, we'd all sing Christmas songs. Everybody showed up, even people that didn't set foot in the church for the rest of the year. That's where we'd meet Grandpa George and Grandma Vic. After the party, they'd come back home with us to spend Christmas. But this year, I knew none of that was gonna happen.

That night we all sat at the table workin' on our school lessons. Frankie wrote down some arithmetic problems on my slate. I tried to do 'em, but the numbers got all jumbled up in my head on account of John talkin' so much.

"What you doin', Roxie?" John asked.

" 'Rithmetic."

"Can I help?"

"No, John."

"Mama, Roxie won't let me help!"

"Mama, make him hush."

Mama plopped him down into her rocker. "Stop pesterin' your sister. She's workin' on her school lessons."

"When I get big, I'm gonna go to school, and I won't let Roxie help me with my 'rithmetic." On and on he went. Finally, I was able to ignore his squawkin' long enough to finish my lessons.

Inez read some more from the Sears & Roebuck catalogue, and then we headed up to bed. As I laid there, I could hear the wind whistlin' through the trees and the steady sleet hittin' against the side of the house. It sounded like bacon fryin'. I covered my head with the quilt to try to drown out the noise. Ruby snuggled up close to me and said, "At least it ain't more snow."

In the mornin', Papa was back at the table sippin' his coffee. "Mornin', Roxie girl."

I was glad he was in much better spirits than the day before. "Mornin', Papa." I went to the window to see what the night had brought. We'd gotten no more snow, and the paths were still cleared. That put me at ease, but the sleet had coated everything with ice. The big tall pine tree glistened in the sunlight. It looked like it was made out of shiny green glass.

The sky was no longer gray, but a clear blue. As I stood there lookin' out, I muttered to myself, "Yeah, I think blue is definitely my favorite color."

Papa came over to join me at the window. "Do you think you'll be able to stand not shovelin' any snow today?"

"I think I'll be able to stand it just fine."

Mama chimed in, "Don't get your hopes up too high, Roxie. Y'all need to clear me a spot so I can build a fire to do the wash."

"That ain't nothin', Mama. After all the snow I've shoveled, that'll be a breeze."

She smiled. "I reckon it will at that, Roxie."

We did the wash once a week, on Tuesdays. Mama would build a fire down by the barn and would put a big black kettle on top of it. Then we'd fill the kettle up with water. While the water in the kettle came to a boil, we'd fill the wash tub with cold water. I reckon nobody has to ask who fetched all that water. Mama would take a cake of soap and wash all the dirty clothes in there. When the water in the kettle was boilin', we'd put clothes in the hot water. They'd soak there for about a half an hour while one of us stirred 'em with a big wooden paddle. Then we'd lift 'em up with the paddle and wring 'em out, once they were cool enough to handle.

After breakfast, us girls went down to the barn to do the wash with Mama. Frank was in the barn workin' with Papa. Mama made John stay in the house. She said that he'd just be in the way.

I was takin' turns stirrin' the wash with Ruby while Mama, Frankie, and Inez scrubbed the clothes with the soap. I was thankful that I didn't have to put my hands in the cold water. Inez brought over one of Papa's shirts and dropped it into the kettle, then stayed a minute to warm her hands by the fire. "Did you see that washin' machine in the catalogue, Mama?"

"I saw it."

"It sure is somethin'. It's electric and practically does the wash for you. It has two rollin' pins that you put the clothes through to get the water out, so you don't have to wring 'em out by hand. Wouldn't you just love to have one of them, Mama?"

"I reckon it'd be nice, 'cept it wouldn't do us much good, considerin' we don't have any electricity."

John came out of the house. "Mama!"

"What is it, Baby John?"

"I just wanted to say 'hey'!"

"'Hey' back to you. Now get in the house and be good for Mama."

"OK!" He went inside.

The breeze started to pick up, and the smoke from the fire blew in my face, makin' my eyes water. I rubbed 'em. "Darn smoke!"

Mama looked over her shoulder. "Don't you swear, Roxie."

"Darn ain't swearin'."

"And don't sass me neither, or I'll wash your mouth out with this soap."

"I'm sorry, Mama, but the smoke was blowin' in my face."

"Well, you know what they say. Smoke follows beauty."

I looked at Ruby. The smoke wasn't blowin' her way. She must've known what I was thinkin', 'cause she shoved the paddle toward me and said, "Your turn to stir."

John came out again. "Mama!"

"What is it now, Baby John?"

"I just wanted to say 'hey' again!"

"'Hey' again back to you."

"And I love you."

"I love you, too. Now get back in the house."

"OK, Mama." He started to go inside, then turned around. "Mama?"

"What, Baby John?"

"How much longer you gonna be?"

"Not much longer."

" 'Cause I miss you!"

"I miss you, too."

"OK!" He went back into the house and closed the door behind him.

"Why do you let him act like that, Mama?" I asked as I stirred the clothes.

"Like what?"

"Like such a baby."

" 'Cause he still *is* a baby. You acted pretty much the same way when you were his age."

I could barely remember back that far, but I was sure that I didn't act like John.

Frankie and Inez dropped the last of the soapy clothes into the kettle. Mama took the paddle out of my hands. "I'll stir for a while. You girls go in the barn until they're ready to be wrung out."

We walked toward the barn door, happy to get in out of the cold wind for a few minutes. When we were almost there, we heard a sound—a groanin', crackin' sound. I turned around. What I saw sent a wave of terror over me. The big tall pine tree had snapped and was fallin' right toward the house. It seemed like minutes, but it was only a few seconds. Then Mama screamed at the top of her lungs, "THE BABY!"

12 · *Crash!*

The tree hit the house and made a loud crash. The next few seconds were all a blur. I remember seein' logs flyin' across the yard and rollin' down the hill. Frankie and Inez ran toward the house, with Mama leadin' the way. The barn door flew open and Papa shouted, "What happened?" Ruby pointed toward the house. Papa's eyes opened wide. Then he was off, goin' as fast as he could, screamin' for Mama as he ran. Frank was right on his heels. I stood there, not able to move or speak. A big puff of smoke rose up from the house and blew away almost as fast as it had risen. Then

Ruby started cryin'. This snapped me out of my stupor, and I ran toward the house, leavin' Ruby there screamin' and sobbin'.

We climbed through the branches of the big pine tree, throwin' chairs and household goods out of our way as we went, each of us calling out, "Baby John! Baby John, where are you?" A couple of minutes later, Frank cried out, "He's here! I found 'em!"

He crawled out through the branches carryin' John. Mama grabbed him out of Frank's arms. "Baby John! Baby John, can you hear me?" His body was limp. He made no sound at all. Mama laid him on the ground. I could see that there was a little cut on his forehead, and a few drops of blood fell down into the snow. "Wake up, Baby John. Can you hear me?" He didn't move. Mama looked up at Papa, tears runnin' down her cheeks. "Bass . . . I think he's . . . I think he's . . ."

Before she could say it, John opened his eyes.

"Hey, Mama, did you finish the washin'? I missed you." Mama started to laugh, then her laughter changed to great sobs. John was still dazed, but he reached up and touched Mama's cheek. "Don't cry, Mama. I'll stay inside and be good." Then he pulled up both arms to give her a hug, and I noticed somethin' peculiar. His left arm looked like it had two elbows, 'cept one went the wrong way. John's face suddenly turned as white as the snow, and he let out a scream. "It hurts! My arm hurts!"

Papa picked him up off the ground. "His arm's broken. Let's get him to the barn." We followed Papa, all of us shaken up from the ordeal. Ruby was still standin' by the barn door cryin'. Inez led her inside. Papa gently laid John down in a bed of hay.

John was cryin' with pain. "Fix it, Papa!"

"I will, Baby John." Then Papa commenced to make things all right. "Inez, get some wood and start a fire."

"Yes, Papa."

The German man who built the barn had worked as a blacksmith. He'd made a little fireplace off to one side. I'd always thought it was kind of useless to have a fireplace in the barn, but now I was about to find out that one could come in real handy.

"Roxie, have you seen any spiderwebs?"

"What?" I asked, confused by his question.

"I need a spiderweb. Do you know where to find one?"

"There's a great big one up in the hayloft. Ruby told me about it. She was skeered to go near it."

"Get it for me."

"What for?"

"Don't ask me any questions, just do what I say. Frank, Frankie, go to the woodshed and dig up a bucket of red clay. You'll have to move the big logs. There's a bank of red clay behind 'em."

Frank and Frankie shot out of the barn like a

flash, and I was up the ladder to the hayloft. As I climbed, I heard Papa say to Ruby, "Now stop cryin'. Go out to your mama's wash and get one of my clean shirts." John had stopped cryin' by now, but Ruby was still ballin' her eyes out.

There was a big black spider hangin' in the web. I picked up a piece of straw and poked at it so it would go away. After several pokins, it climbed up the wall. Before I pulled down the web, I looked up at the spider. "Papa needs this. Sorry I have to tear your house down. I know how it feels."

I shimmied down the ladder with the spiderweb in my hand just as Ruby came back into the barn. She had finally stopped cryin'. Papa took the wet shirt and ripped off a piece. He used it to clean the blood off of John's forehead, but some blood still trickled out from the cut and ran into John's hair. "Hand me that spiderweb, Roxie." He wadded it and put it on the cut. It turned red with the blood.

Then he wiped away the trickle that led to John's hair. The bleedin' stopped. Papa looked at me. "To answer your question, that's what the spider-web's for."

Frank and Frankie came back in with the bucket of red clay. We broke it up and picked out every stick, twig, and pebble. Papa got some hot water from Mama's wash kettle and poured it into the bucket. He squished the clay around with his fingers. It looked like he was makin' biscuits, same as me and Mama had done. "Ruby, get me some clean straw." He added it to the mixture and squished it some more. He got two pieces of flat wood and wiped 'em off with part of the shirt. Then he went over to John. "We'll have you fixed up in no time at all, Baby John."

He gently lifted John's arm and took him by the hand. Then he gave the arm a yank, snappin' the bone back into place.

John didn't cry one bit. Instead, he took his good arm and slapped Papa hard across the face. "What did you wanna go and do that for, Papa?"

Papa didn't answer John, but he looked at me and said, "Well, I reckon I can't say I blame him for doin' that."

Papa took the two pieces of flat wood and placed 'em on each side of John's arm to make a splint, tying 'em together with twine. He tore off more of the shirt and wrapped it around the splint. Then he got the bucket and spread the clay mixture over the whole thing to make a cast.

"Good boy, Baby John, you were real brave."

"I know I was."

Papa put him by the fire. "You stay here so it'll dry. I'll put on another layer when it does."

Then I noticed Mama standin' in the shadows. There was a small window near her, and it cast a little bit of light on her face. I realized that she hadn't said a word or even moved from that spot since we came into the barn. I walked over to her. Part of her bun had come loose, and the hair was hangin' down at one side. Her face was covered with red splotches, and her eyes were puffy from cryin'. All of a sudden, she didn't look young anymore. In fact, she looked almost as old as Grandma Vic. I took her by the hand. "He's all right now, Mama. Baby John's gonna be just fine." I led her over to the fireplace, and she lowered herself to the ground, puttin' her arm around John.

Then she looked up at Papa and asked in a weak voice, "What are we gonna do now, Bass?"

He went to the door and looked out at the house. "There's only one thing to do. We're movin' into the barn."

13 · *Switchin' Places*

I fetched a bucket of water for Mama while the others brought in the wash. She cleaned up John and fixed her hair. Then she splashed cold water on her face. The red splotches faded away, and soon she looked like herself again.

Mama and Ruby stayed to take care of John and began to clean up the barn while the rest of us made our way up to the house, or at least what was left of it. The side wall was completely knocked down, and so was part of the roof and the top of the chimney. Lucky for us, clumps of snow had put out the fire, or everything might've burned. The big tall pine tree laid spread out across the floor.

Papa went into the house to check the roof. He wanted to make sure that the rest of it wasn't gonna fall on us. Then he let out a deep breath and said, "Well, let's get to it." We climbed through the branches and began cartin' everything down to the barn.

Most of the furniture was still fine, but the table had been busted in half, and two of the chairs were smashed. I figured the chairs didn't matter, seein' as how we wouldn't be havin' company anytime soon.

It took us several hours, but we got the house emptied out. We piled everything into the main part of the barn. The heavy woodstove was the last thing that we brought in. Ruby and Mama had cleaned up most of the loose hay and straw by that time. Mama was makin' bean soup in the fireplace, bakin' bread and roastin' taters in the hot coals. Papa took the door of the house off its hinges and brought it down to the barn. He put it on top of two sawhorses. That was gonna be our table now that the other one was busted. We sat down to eat.

Papa had put more layers of clay on John's arm and had made him a sling out of the rest of the shirt. John didn't cry anymore, but he complained that he had trouble eatin' with just one hand. So Mama cut up his tater and helped him out. He thought it was great fun to be eatin' in the barn, but he was the only one who felt that way.

When we finished supper, it was startin' to get dark. Papa called Frank and Frankie into the part of the barn where the stalls were. A few minutes later, they came back out leadin' the cows and mules behind 'em.

As they headed out the door, Mama asked, "Where are you goin' with the cows and mules, Bass?"

As he went out the door, he looked over his

shoulder and said, "Just never you mind, Callie."

Mama walked over to the window to see where they were goin'. Then she turned around with both hands on her hips. "Well, goodness to heavens! Here my youngins are livin' in the barn, and your Papa's movin' the cows and mules into the house!" Then she burst out laughin'. It felt awful good to hear it, after hearin' her cryin' and screamin' earlier in the day. We laughed, too.

We put Mama and Papa's rope bed in one of the stalls and laid the fluffy feather tick on top of it. Us youngins slept on ticks that were filled with straw. Frank's tick was put in the second stall, Inez and Frankie's was in the third, and Ruby and me would be sleepin' up in the loft, just like we did in the house. Mama set her rocker next to the fireplace and told us that everything else could wait till tomorrow. Then she sent us off to bed.

As we dressed for bed, Ruby asked me, "Reckon

why that tree fell on the house?"

" 'Cause it was old, and all the snow and ice was too much weight on it."

"Oh." She waited a minute, then spoke again. "I thought Baby John was dead for sure. I was awful skeered."

"I know you were. You were cryin' up a storm."

"I was not!" I just looked at her, and she said, "Well, maybe I cried a little bit." She pulled her nightshirt over her head. "You know what, Roxie? Between diggin' out paths and trees fallin' on us, this snow is liable to kill us."

"That's one of the first sensible things I've ever heard you say, Ruby Dockery." She huffed at me and jumped into bed.

"That's my side of the bed, Ruby!" I said, shooin' her over. She was always tryin' to take my side of the bed. The piece of blue print from my store-bought dress was sewn into the quilt on my side. "Now move." She huffed again and scooted over as I crawled under the covers.

Mama turned down the lamp and the light grew dim. Then she started singin' soft and low to put John to sleep.

> *Hush a bye, don't you cry,*
> *Go to sleep, my little baby.*
> *When you wake,*
> *You'll have cake,*
> *And all the pretty horses.*

I laid there listenin' to her sing, thinkin' about all the tears that she'd cried that day. I thought about how pitiful John looked laying there in the snow with the blood runnin' out of his forehead. I felt guilty that I'd fussed so when John was actin' like such a baby. I would've never said a word against him if I'd known that a few seconds later, he'd have a tree fallin' on him. And I made up my mind right then that I'd try not to say bad things against anybody, whether trees were about to fall on 'em or not.

The smell of the sweet straw made me think about the candy that we wouldn't be gettin' this Christmas. In the darkness, I moved my hand to the patch of blue print and tried to think nice thoughts as I drifted to sleep.

14 · *Be It Ever So Humble, There's No Place Like a Barn*

The next day, we set out to fix up the barn. There was lots of cleanin' to be done. We had to make sure that there was no hay or straw anywhere near the fire, or the place might burn down. Papa said that if it did, we'd have to move to the outhouse.

Papa had Frank go with him to take down the plank shelves in the kitchen part of the house so they could put 'em up in the barn. After that, they went to work settin' up the woodstove so Mama wouldn't have to cook in the fireplace anymore.

The bottom of the barn walls was made out

of big rocks goin' up about four feet high. Above the rocks were thick logs, like the house was made out of. So Papa couldn't cut a hole in the wall to fit the stovepipe through. Instead, he was takin' out one of the pieces of glass from the window so he could put the pipe through there. Mama said that suited her just fine, 'cause that way she'd have plenty of light to see by when she cooked supper.

John was bein' good and didn't complain or bother us much while we worked. He sat at the table and drew pictures on my slate. "Look, Mama, I drew the tree that fell on me."

"That's real pretty, Baby John," Mama said.

I looked at the slate. All I saw was a bunch of squiggles, but I didn't argue. If it looked like a tree to him, I'd let it be a tree.

Frankie was sweepin', and she had been for a while. She stopped and leaned on the broom.

"Mama, I feel like the craziest person that ever walked the face of the earth!"

"Well, I'm sure there are lots of people that are crazier than you. But why do you feel that way, Frankie?"

" 'Cause I'm sweepin' dirt!"

"What do you wanna do with dirt—eat it?"

"That ain't what I mean, Mama. The floor's made out of dirt, not wood. I feel like a fool sweepin' dirt. When am I supposed to stop? When I sweep myself all the way down to China?"

"Well, you've always wanted to travel."

"Oh, Mama!"

"Just sweep until there's no more loose dirt. Now get back to work."

"Yes, Mama."

I'd been puttin' stuff on the shelves with Ruby, and we had just finished. I sat down at the table for a minute. "Mama?"

"Yes, Roxie?"

"Me and Ruby were havin' an argument this mornin'."

"You don't mean it! You and Ruby arguin'? I find that hard to believe."

Papa was still fixin' the stovepipe. He chuckled at what Mama had said. I went over to where she was workin'. "We were tryin' to figure out what to call this place. I say we ought to still call it the barn. Ruby says we ought to call it the house."

Mama thought on this for a moment. "Well, there's no denying that this is a barn, but it's also gonna be our home for a while. But that's just until the snow melts and your Papa can start buildin' a new house. So, how about for now we call it . . . the Christmas barn?"

John jumped up from the table and started shoutin', "Christmas candy! Christmas candy! I can't wait for Santa to bring us Christmas candy!"

Mama carried him over to her rocker. "Now, Baby John, maybe Santa won't be able to make it this year, what with all of this snow."

"That won't matter, Mama. Santa's got mules that can fly. Didn't you know that?" That made all of us laugh—well, all of us except for Papa.

Papa got a strange look on his face and stopped workin'. "There you go, Callie, the stove's put up." He went over to John. "Let me have a look at that arm." He got more mud from the bucket to patch up the cracks that had formed in the cast.

When he was done, he sat down at the table and stayed real quiet. I could tell that he was deep in thought. John kept on chattering about Christmas candy and Santa. We tried to make him hush, but this was John we're talkin' about. Papa got up from the table, picked up the piece of glass that he had taken out of the window, and started for the door. "I've got some work to do in the woodshed. I need to move those big logs back."

Frank followed him. "I'll help you, Papa."

"No, I'll do it myself. You stay here and help your Mama." Then he was out the door.

After he'd gone, Frank looked at Mama. "Since when is he so all fired set to move logs?"

"I don't know, Frank. Maybe he just wants a little time to himself. Now come over here and help me hang up the washtub."

We all went back to work, scrubbin' and cleanin', movin' things this way and that. Inez put Mama's dried flowers around the room to give the place a little color and to brighten things up. Frankie hung the calendars on the wall near the door. There were three of 'em. At the bottom of each calendar was written "Compliments of Bryson's Grain and Feed." Each had a picture of a bird perched up on a tree branch. On the 1928 calendar was a bluebird. The 1929 one had a cardinal. This year's was two hummingbirds, one on a tree branch and the other hoverin' in the air. Mama loved to have pictures on the walls, but we had to make do with the calendars since they were the only pictures we had. Sometimes us youngins would tear pages out of the Sears & Roebuck catalogue and put 'em up. But Mama would pull 'em down and say, "Take those down, they look like a mess!"

After a couple more hours, we were finished. We looked around the room. Inez sat down in Mama's rocker. "It ain't so bad after all."

Frankie agreed. "In fact, except for the dirt floor, I think it's better than the house was." We all thought so. There was lots more room, and the German man had built the place real sturdy. The house was half gone, but the barn sat solid on its foundation of big gray stones.

I thought about those mules again and asked,

"Mama, why in the world have the mules been livin' better than we've been livin'?"

15 · *An Idea in the Barn— I Mean the House*

I t was time to feed the animals and do the milkin', so we all headed up to the barn— I mean the house. It was still confusin'. Whenever we were outside and Mama would say, "Roxie, go the barn and do this," or "Roxie, go to the house and do that," I would keep goin' the wrong way.

I stood in front of one of the mules, lookin' into his big brown eyes. I reached up and rubbed the soft hair on his nose. Then I got real close to one of his long, pointed ears. "Ha, ha, ha, we're livin' in the barn now."

He huffed just like Ruby did whenever I said somethin' that she didn't like. Frank and Frankie came into the barn—I mean the house. They carried in food for the mules and the cows: two big basketfuls of hay, seed corn, and corn shucks. Frank started feedin' the mules.

Frankie sat down on the spot where the stove used to be. "I was just thinkin' about somethin'."

Inez was headin' into Mama and Papa's old room to start milkin' the cows. "What's that, Frankie?"

"Well, I understand about Papa not bein' able to get into town to get us anything for Christmas, but—"

Inez cut her off. "Well, he can't help that."

"Oh, I don't mind. A couple sticks of candy ain't really that big of a deal anyway. Especially for me. I'm fifteen now. But he won't be gettin' anything for Mama. That bothers me."

When they went into town for Christmas things,

Papa would always slip off and get somethin' for Mama. It wouldn't be much—maybe a couple of handkerchiefs or somethin' like that.

Frankie leaned back against the wall. "I sure do wish I could get her somethin' out of that catalogue. If we could get her somethin' out of there, what do you reckon she'd like?"

Frank picked up a handful of corn shucks and gave 'em to the mule. "There ain't no point in thinkin' about it, 'cause it ain't gonna happen."

We weren't gonna let him spoil our dreamin'. Inez put down the milk bucket. "I still think she'd like that washin' machine—that is, if we had electricity."

Ruby chirped up. "She told Baby John that she was partial to the stick pony. But I don't think she really meant it."

I sat down beside Frankie to give my thoughts. "I saw her lookin' at pictures of hats. Remember when she used to wear hats to church?"

Inez picked up the bucket. "Yeah, but they're all worn out now."

Frank grabbed another bunch of corn shucks and gave 'em to the mule. "It's like I said before, there ain't no point in thinkin' about it. We can't get her a hat or nothin' else."

Inez looked annoyed at Frank and started through the doorway. Then she stopped. "Maybe we can, Frank."

"Can what?" he asked.

"Get her a hat. I can make her one. Grandma Vic showed me how to make 'em the summer I stayed with her. I can make it out of corn shucks. It'll look almost like a straw hat."

I got up off the ground. "How long will it take?"

"Just a couple of hours if you all help. Roxie, slip into the house and get me two needles, some white thread, white cloth, and the scissors out of Mama's sewin' basket. But don't let her see you. Frank,

Frankie, go through those corn shucks and pull out some nice big ones. Ones that don't have any spots on 'em. Ruby, go to the pump and get me a bucket of water."

"But that's Roxie's job!"

"Do you wanna help or not?"

"Oh, all right."

We were all off to follow Inez's instructions. When we came back, she told us what to do. First, we soaked the corn shucks in the water. Then she cut 'em into little squares and we folded 'em over once and then over again, makin' each one into a triangle.

Next, she cut the white cloth into the right shapes. She made a circle about the size of a flapjack. Then she cut another bigger circle with a hole in the middle of it, like an "O." The third piece was a long, narrow strip. Then she and Frankie sewed all the little triangles in rows onto the cloth while the rest of us watched and talked.

I paid close attention to Inez as she worked. I studied her every move so I'd know how to make hats, too. "Mama sure is gonna be surprised." Then I had a different thought. "What about Papa, Inez? Shouldn't we have a present for him?"

"I don't think he'd like one of these hats, Roxie."

"Why don't we do somethin' else for him?"

"Like what?" Inez asked.

"Well, maybe we could all work extra hard for him the week after Christmas."

Frankie looked up from her sewin'. "If we work any harder then we have for the past few days, we'll all be dead by the new year."

Then Ruby had a thought. "How about a shirt? He tore up one of his to fix Baby John's arm, remember? Frankie could make it for him. Couldn't you, Frankie?"

"I'm afraid I don't have enough cloth all the

same color to make a shirt big enough for Papa."

Ruby thought for a minute. "I know! You could use my brown dress! Roxie has one just like it. If you cut up both of 'em, do you think you'd have enough?"

"Well, I reckon. Would you mind, Roxie?"

"No, I wouldn't mind." After all, it wasn't a blue print dress. "But what about Mama—do you think she'll care?"

Frank answered me. "She won't as long as it's somethin' for Papa. But Frankie, do you think you can finish it before Christmas?"

"I think so, if I work on it in here when we take care of the mules. And I can work on it some more at night when I go to bed, as long as Mama don't make me put out the lamp."

Inez stitched the three pieces together, and the hat was finished. We all stepped back to look at it. Frank cocked his head to one side. "Ain't the top a little lopsided?"

"It'll straighten itself out when it dries," Inez said, defendin' her work. "I think."

I moved close to her side, amazed at this hidden talent that she had. "It's real pretty, Inez. It looks like a great big flower."

"That's what I said to Grandma Vic when she taught me how to make 'em."

We all stood there admirin' the hat. Even the mule seemed pleased. He lowered his neck to inspect Inez's handiwork. He gave it a sniff. And before we knew what that mule was doin', Mama's hat was in his mouth, and he was chompin' it up for dessert. Frank leaped toward him. "No!"

Frank tried to get the hat back, but the mule swallowed, and it was gone. Frank raised his hand to give the mule a slap across the head, but Inez grabbed his arm before he could. "No, Frank! He didn't know any better! After all, they were his corn shucks in the first place. I'll just make another one tomorrow. Besides, that one was lopsided."

We all went back to the house—I mean the barn, draggin' our tails behind us. Frank noticed Mama comin' up from the woodshed. "I'll go down to the shed and get you some firewood, Mama."

"There's no need. Your papa's already brought some up. Instead, you can fetch me some water."

That cheered me up. First Ruby had to get water and now Frank, all in the same twenty-four hours. It wasn't even my birthday.

It was startin' to get dark, and we were about to sit down to supper when Papa came in. Mama went to take his coat. "Supper's ready, Bass."

"Keep somethin' warm for me, Callie. I'll eat it later." He took the lantern off the hook and went back outside.

Frank looked puzzled. "Mama, is somethin' the matter with Papa?"

"I reckon he's just got a case of the blues on account of all the snow. Now let's sit down and eat."

Supper came and went, and Papa still hadn't come in. We did our lessons and spent some time with the Sears & Roebuck catalogue. We were up to page one hundred and twenty-two when Mama said the usual, "It's bedtime." We didn't ask to stay up tonight. Well, none of us except for Frankie.

"Mama, can I have the sewin' basket?"

"What for?"

"I need to fix up Roxie and Ruby's brown dresses. They're gettin' worn out."

"Tonight? You wanna work on 'em tonight?"

"Well, it might take me a while. They're in pretty bad shape. Besides, I ain't sleepy yet."

Mama gave her the sewin' basket while we all watched. "What are y'all lookin' at?"

"Nothin', Mama."

"Nothin', Mama."

"Nothin', Mama."

"Nothin', Mama."

"If you ain't lookin' at nothin', then get to bed like I told you to!"

"Yes, Mama."

"Yes, Mama."

"Yes, Mama."

"Yes, Mama."

Inez and Frank ran into their stalls; me and Ruby scurried up the ladder. Once we were up, Frankie shouted, "Roxie, throw those brown dresses down so I can fix 'em." I tossed 'em out of the loft and Frankie caught 'em. I gave her a wink, and she winked back at me.

She gave Mama a kiss on the cheek and said, "Night-night, Mama." Then she went into her stall.

I watched Mama as she carried John off to put him to sleep. "Night-night, Mama."

"Night-night, Roxie."

I was takin' off my dress to get ready for bed when Ruby asked, "Why do you reckon Papa didn't come back?"

"I don't know. I suppose it's like Mama said, he must have the blues on account of the snow."

"Do you think it's 'cause he can't get us anything for Christmas?"

"I don't know."

"He'll get cheered up when we give him the shirt."

"I reckon." I turned to get into the bed. "Move, that's my side of the bed." She gave me her usual huff and scooted over.

We laid there sayin' nothin', but I knew that we were both thinkin' about the same thing. Then Ruby raised up. "Mama!"

"What, Ruby?"

"Don't worry if Frankie has the lamp on

for just a little while!"

"I won't, Ruby."

Then she laid back down. After a moment, she raised up again. " 'Cause she's fixin' our brown dresses, that's all!"

From under the covers, I took my foot and gave her a hard kick. Ruby hollered, "Ouch! Why did you do that?"

" 'Cause you're a blabbermouth, Ruby!" I whispered.

Mama called out, "What's goin' on up there?"

"Nothin', Mama," I hollered. "Ruby just stubbed her toe when she was gettin' in the bed!"

Then I lowered my voice to a whisper. "Now hush up, or Mama's gonna suspect somethin', blabbermouth." Ruby kept quiet after that and went to sleep.

I stayed awake for a while listenin' for Papa to come in. Mama started singin' to John, the same lullaby she'd always sing to him. The last words I uttered that night were, "Stupid Ruby . . . stupid mule."

16 · *Corn Shucks?*

When I woke up, I saw that Ruby had already gotten out of bed. So I got dressed real quick and headed down the ladder before she would have a chance to blab about the shirt to Mama. Ruby was sittin' at the table playin' with John, and Mama was gettin' breakfast ready.

"Mornin', Mama."

"How'd you sleep, Roxie?"

"Good, Mama."

Frank came out of his stall. "Mornin', everybody." He saw that the fire was blazing and more big logs were layin' by the hearth. "Who brought in more firewood?"

"Your papa," Mama said.

"But why?"

"Well, I reckon he was cold."

"Where is he?"

"He was out early this mornin'."

Frank took the chair next to mine. "Is Papa mad at us about somethin'? I didn't do anythin' that I can think of."

"Me neither," I added.

John wasn't about to be left out. "Not me neither!"

Mama pulled the biscuits out of the oven and slammed the pan down onto the table. "No, he ain't mad, but I'm gonna be if you don't stop askin' me all these questions. Roxie, go in and wake up Frankie. She was up half the night workin' on those dresses. I finally had to go in there and make her get in the bed." She went back to the stove to stir the sausage gravy.

Ruby looked at me. Her eyes were opened wide. "You went in there, Mama?"

"That's what I said."

"What did you see? What was she doin'? She wasn't doin' nothin', was she?" I reached under the table and gave Ruby a harder kick than I had the night before. "Ouch!"

Mama turned around. "What's the matter?"

"Oh, nothin', Mama," Ruby said, shootin' me a look. "I just stubbed my toe again."

"Well, be careful. We've had enough broken bones to do us for a while."

As I went in to wake up Frankie, I looked at Ruby and mouthed the word "blabbermouth."

We got through breakfast without Ruby givin' away our secrets, but we sat on pins and needles while we ate. We all glared at her, darin' her to speak. After we finished, we went to take care of the animals and see to our chores. At least that's what we told Mama.

We were gone for most of the day, and she was glad to be rid of us. All of our questions about Papa were drivin' her out of her head. Frankie managed to get out with the sewin' basket without Mama seein' her. She worked on Papa's shirt while me and Inez made Mama's hat. Frank and Ruby did most of our chores so that we could finish. Ruby didn't like that, but she didn't complain too much.

Frankie had finished the main part of the shirt and had made the sleeves, but she hadn't attached 'em yet. She held it up to show us her progress. "How does it look?"

"It's real nice, Frankie," Inez said as she looked up from her own work.

I agreed. Ruby walked over and examined the shirt carefully. "You'd never know it used to be our dresses."

Frankie laughed. "Well, that's a good thing. Papa would sure look funny walkin' around in one of your dresses."

Frankie went back to her sewin'. "I sure do hate makin' buttonholes. They're the hardest part."

Inez put the three parts of the hat together and stitched some of Mama's dried flowers around the brim. "There, it's finished."

I looked over at the mule and clenched my teeth. "Don't you even dare to think about it."

Frank came over to take a look at the hat. "That's a lot better than the last one. It ain't lopsided at all. I reckon it's a good thing the mule ate the other one. Hey, Frankie, if the shirt don't turn out so good, why don't you give it to the mule?"

Ruby laughed, but Frankie didn't think it was very funny. "It'd better turn out. I've worked my fingers to the bone. Come here, Frank, and put it on so I can attach the sleeves."

Frank put on the shirt and buttoned it up. "Hey, Frankie, this button ain't the same as the others."

"Do you think Papa will notice?"

Frank knew that he'd better not say so. "Nah, they're all white. That's close enough."

Frankie stitched the sleeves on while Frank stood there wearin' Papa's big brown shirt. It hung down almost to his knees, and the sleeves went past his fingertips. It made him look like he wasn't much bigger than John. "Ouch, Frankie, you stuck me!"

"Well, hold still and I won't. And don't get any blood on the shirt or I'll have to wash it," Frankie scolded.

"Well, if that don't beat all. I'm standin' here bleedin', and you're worried about havin' to wash a shirt!"

Before long, the sleeves were attached. "Now it's beginnin' to look like somethin'. You can take it off now, Frank. I'll put the collar on tonight, and it'll be finished."

We headed back to the barn. I'd gotten it straight in my head by that time. Frank stopped and looked down toward the woodshed. "I think I'll go and get Mama some firewood."

Frankie grabbed him by the coat. "You'd better not, Frank. Mama said that Papa wanted to be alone."

"That was yesterday. Besides, I'll ask before I go into the shed." We all followed Frank down the hill. At the bottom, he stopped. "Papa?" There was no answer. "Papa, are you in there?" Still no answer. "I thought I'd come down and get Mama some firewood." The door opened, but just a little bit. A big log came flyin' out and landed in the snow, then another one and another one. Then the door closed.

Frankie looked at Frank. "See, I told you so." We gathered up the wood and headed back to the barn.

When we got inside, Mama asked, "Where did you get that wood?"

Frank put his log down on the hearth. "Papa threw 'em out in the snow."

"Oh." Then she went to the stove to work. She had her back to us, and she said, "Frank."

"Yeah, Mama?"

"I want you to go get me some corn shucks, nice big ones that don't have any spots on 'em."

We stood there frozen. Then Ruby asked, "What do you want with corn shucks? You ain't plannin' to make a—" This time I kicked one leg and Inez kicked the other. "Ouch."

Mama turned around. "What's the matter, Ruby, did you stub your toe again?"

"Yeah, Mama, both of 'em this time."

"Well, try to be more careful. Frank, I believe I asked you to do somethin'. Don't just stand there. Do what I said."

"Yes, Mama."

When Frank came back with the corn shucks, Mama put 'em in a pan of water to soak. We all stared at her while she did this. I pulled Inez aside and told her that we didn't know for certain that Mama was plannin' to make a hat, and that even if she did, she could always use two of 'em. This brought her a little comfort, but I could tell that she was just as worried as I was.

When Mama was nearly finished makin' supper, the door opened and Papa came in. "Hey, youngins, where've you been hidin' yourselves? I ain't seen you all day."

Frank looked at me and hunched his shoulders, then looked back at Papa. "Nowhere, Papa."

We were all relieved to know that Papa wasn't mad at us. John ran to him and jumped up into his arms. "Hey, Papa!"

"Hey, Baby John, how's that arm?"

"It's broke, Papa. Did you forget?"

Papa let out a laugh that seemed to shake the whole barn. Then he put John down in a chair. "Come with me, Frank. I need you to help me do somethin'." Frank put on his coat, and they left the barn.

Inez was settin' the table, I was helpin' Mama cook, Ruby was keepin' John occupied, and Frankie had slipped off to her stall when the door flew open. Mama looked up and let out a gasp. "What in the world are you doin', Bass?"

17 · *The Return of the Big Tall Pine*

Papa and Frank came into the barn, draggin' the pine tree behind 'em. "What does it look like I'm doin'? I'm bringin' in this here tree."

Mama took off her apron. "What in the world are you doin' that for?"

"Well, they'll be decoratin' the tree at the church tonight, and seein' as how we can't get there, I thought we'd have our own tree decoratin' here in the barn. Frank, let's set her up on the other side of the room."

Papa had cut off the top part of the tree, about eight feet of it. The whole tree was about thirty feet tall to begin with. He'd nailed two boards to the bottom so it would stand up on its own. They put the pine in the corner by Frank's stall. "There, I think she'll make a right nice Christmas tree, don't you, Callie?"

"I'd think you would've had enough of that old pine tree by now."

"Well, we might as well get some good out of it, after all the trouble it's caused us."

We ate our supper in a flash so that we could get to decoratin' the tree. None of us was much hungry. We were too excited. But Mama made all of us clean our plates. While we ate, every once in a while John would get up and go over to the tree. He'd give it a kick or a slap and say, "Serves you right for breakin' my arm. Stupid old tree!"

After we'd washed the dishes, we sat down to make the tree decorations. Mama mixed up some flour, salt, and water to make a paste. "How far are you youngins in that catalogue?"

Inez got the book. "We're up to page one hundred and twenty-two." Mama took the book and ripped off that part. She got the scissors, and Frankie cut some of the pages into little strips. She and Ruby used the paste to glue the strips and make chains. John tried to help, but he was just makin' a mess and kept tryin' to eat the paste. Mama gave him my slate and told him to draw her another picture of the tree.

Mama took the rest of the pages from the catalogue and showed me and Inez how to fold 'em so they looked like little birds. As we sat there foldin', it made me think about foldin' the corn shucks. I leaned over to Inez and whispered, "I'm sure she ain't makin' a hat."

Frank popped some poppin' corn in the kettle on the fireplace. He and Papa got needles and thread and tried to string the popcorn, but they both kept stickin' their fingers. Frankie said that she and Ruby would take over for 'em, and they could work on makin' the chains. Frank whispered to Frankie, "Good. Between this and you stickin' me with a needle all afternoon, I'm liable to go to bed without a drop of blood left in my body."

We put the little birds, the chains, and the popcorn strings on the tree. Mama stuck bunches of her dried flowers here and there. When it was all decorated, Papa stood back with his arm around Mama, lookin' at the tree. "You know, most all the people in Murphy put up a tree in their houses. I always thought it was kind of silly. Trees belong in the woods. But now, I gotta admit, I don't think it's silly at all."

Mama started to sing a Christmas song, and we all joined in, just like we did once the tree was decorated at the church. We sang one song after another until we were all dead tired. We were startin' off to bed when Papa got my slate and erased John's picture of the tree.

"Papa, you wiped my picture away," John cried out.

"Don't worry, Baby John," Papa said. "You can draw another one tomorrow. Frankie?"

"Yes, Papa?"

"I want you to put your name down here on this slate."

"What for?"

"I just wanna see what it looks like. I've been thinkin' about learnin' how to read, and I thought it might help me if I was to look at your name. I'd know what it said, and it might help me figure out some of the letters."

"But why my name?"

"Well, I thought I'd start with yours and Frank's, since you two are the oldest. As I figure it, Frank and Frankie ought to look just about the same. Except yours says "e."

"My name has an 'i-e' at the end. Do you want me to write down both of 'em, so you can see the difference?"

"No, yours will do fine for now. I don't want too many letters floatin' around in my head just yet." I could tell that Frankie thought it was a strange thing for him to ask her to do, but she did it anyway. "Now, just put down Frankie. Don't write the Dockery part." He picked up the slate and looked at the letters. "Now, that says Frankie and nothin' else, right?"

"That's right, Papa."

He took the lantern and went outside. "Night, youngins."

Mama closed the door behind him, then turned around. "Frankie."

"Yes, Mama?"

"I'll be needin' my sewin' basket. Are you

· 131 ·

almost finished with it?"

"Yes, Mama, I'll get it for you. I just need a
needle and some thread to finish up."

Ruby was standin' next to me and opened her
big blabbermouth. "Frankie needs the needle and
thread so she can finish fixin' our dresses. That's all
and there's nothin' else to it." Then she quickly
climbed up the ladder so she wouldn't stub her toe
again.

After everyone had gone to bed, me and Ruby
laid on the floor up in the loft lookin' down at the
Christmas tree. I could just make out some of the
decorations in the firelight. Ruby hung her head
over the edge of the planks to get a better look.
"It sure is pretty, ain't it, Roxie? I think it looks
nicer than the one at church last year. I thought I
was gonna miss not goin' to the tree decoratin'
party, but I think this one was better, 'cause it was
just the family." Then she got quiet for a minute.

" 'Cept Grandma and Grandpa didn't get to come back home with us this year."

"Let's not think about that," I said. "Come on, Ruby. Let's get to bed." She sprang to her feet and leaped in. I said the usual, "You're on my side of the bed." She huffed, and then she scooted.

18 · *A Close Call*

Papa was gone again when the mornin' came. The fire was a-blazin' and more logs had been placed by the hearth, the same as the day before. Frank was more puzzled than ever. I told him not to question it, just to be glad that he had one less chore to attend to. Then I went over and sat at the table beside Ruby to wait for breakfast.

John was sittin' across from us, drawin' on my slate, when Frankie came in. She stretched and wiped the sleep out of her eyes. "Mornin', Mama."

John held up the slate. "Look, Frankie." He had drawn the same squiggles that he always drew.

"That's nice, Baby John. That's a real pretty tree."

"That ain't no tree. It's your name, silly."

Mama put a jar of preserves on the table and went back to the stove. "You didn't stay up too late again last night, did you, Frankie?"

"No, Mama, just about an hour."

"Did you finish fixin' the dresses?"

"Yeah, they're all done, every last stitch." Frankie looked me and winked. I winked back.

Then Mama turned to Frankie. "Well, bring 'em in here so I can have a look at 'em."

All of a sudden it seemed like there was no air left in the room, and my palms started sweatin'. I swallowed hard. "You want her to bring 'em in here?"

"That's what I said, Roxie."

Frankie started twirlin' a piece of her hair with one finger and was lookin' real nervous. "You mean you want me to bring 'em in here right now?"

"No, Frankie, I want you to bring 'em in here

next February the seventeenth. Course I mean right now!"

Frankie looked down at the ground, tryin' to come up with somethin' to say. "Well, they didn't turn out all that nice."

Mama put her hand on her hip and tilted her head to one side. "Don't be modest, Frankie. I've seen you do some amazin' things with a needle and thread. Now go get 'em." Frankie just stood there. "What's wrong with you, child?"

"Nothin', Mama."

"Oh, just forget it," We were all relieved, but just for a second. "I'll go get 'em myself."

Mama started toward Frankie's stall. I had to do somethin'. So I hauled off and kicked Ruby in the foot harder than I'd ever kicked anything in my whole life. "Ouch!!!" she hollered.

I jumped up from my chair. "Mama, Ruby stubbed her toe again! Real bad. I think she might've broke it this time. You'd better come over here and take a look at it."

Mama took off Ruby's shoe and examined her foot. "What's gotten into you, Ruby? I've never seen anybody stub their toe so much in my life. It ain't broken." She rubbed Ruby's foot for a minute. "There, does it feel better now?"

"Yeah, Mama."

Mama forgot all about the dresses and went back to gettin' breakfast ready. I whispered to Ruby, "Sorry, but I had to do somethin'."

She whispered back, "Why didn't you stub your own toe?"

" 'Cause Mama wouldn't have believed it. I ain't as clumsy as you are." Of course, Ruby huffed.

It was the day before Christmas and that had us all stirred up, but it was also Friday and that put a damper on things for me. 'Cause Friday was bath day. That meant I'd be fetchin' bucket after bucket of water to fill the washtub.

Mama would build a fire in the yard under the big black kettle to heat the water, and pots and pans were filled up and heated on the stove and in the fireplace. We'd pour the warm water into the washtub for our baths. Mama hung an old bedsheet in one corner of the room for privacy, and we all took our turns. First Frank, then Frankie. After Frankie, Inez. Then me and Ruby's turn together. We were still small enough to both fit in the tub at the same time. Takin' a bath with Ruby suited me just fine, 'cause we changed the water after each bath. It meant one less time that I had to fill the tub. Mama would wash John, then herself. Papa would always be the last.

Papa came back to the barn around two o'clock for his bath. He brought firewood with him, as usual. We sat around the table while he soaked in the tub. From behind the sheet, we could hear him splashin' around and singin':

I saw three ships come sailin' in,
come sailin' in, come sailin' in,
I saw three ships come sailin' in
On Christmas Day in the mornin'.
Bom bom bom bom bom bom bom bom,
Bom bom bom bom, bom bom bom bom,
Bom bom bom bom bom bom bom bom,
On Christmas Day in the mornin'.

After he was finished, he came out from behind the sheet, pullin' his suspenders up over his shoulders. His face was pink from the hot water and the lye soap. He went over to Mama and wrapped his big arms around her. "Do I smell good, woman?"

Mama tried to push him away. "You smell like lye soap, that's all. And don't call me woman!"

"You just don't know how lucky you are to have such a big, strong, good-smellin' man. Why, if it weren't for all this snow, I'd go out and find me another woman."

"Well, the spring thaw will be here soon enough. You can go find yourself another woman then. Now let go of me so I can get back to work."

Papa laughed hard. Then he turned to Frank. "Come with me, boy. You and me's goin' huntin'."

Frank grabbed his coat and darted out the door. "Yes, sir!"

Us girls went up to do the milkin' and feed the mules. Frankie sat down beside me and said, "I was for sure and certain that Mama was gonna make me bring out those dresses. I didn't know what I was gonna do. Thanks, Roxie, that was real quick thinkin'."

Ruby chimed in, "I helped too, you know! I've got the bruises to prove it."

Inez comforted her by sayin', "We know you did, Ruby. You were a big help."

"Thanks, Inez. I just wish bein' a big help didn't have to hurt so much."

We were just about finished fixin' supper when Papa and Frank came back. Papa came through the door carryin' the big wild turkey they'd gotten. "Here's your Christmas dinner, woman. Maybe now you'll appreciate your big strong man."

Mama had to laugh and said, "I appreciate him. Least I do now that he's brought me a great big turkey."

Papa shoved the big bird into Mama's hands. "Well, I thought about gettin' you a panther, but I figured that was woman's work." Then he kissed her.

19 · *Christmas Eve*

We finished our supper. It was just bean soup, roasted taters, and bread again. Mama was takin' it easy since she'd be cookin' a big Christmas dinner the next day.

When we finished, it was time for our entertainment. But tonight, there'd be no readin' from the Sears & Roebuck catalogue. Tonight was Christmas Eve, and we were in for somethin' special.

Inez brought out one of her books. She had about a dozen or more that belonged to her. That ain't countin' her schoolbooks. This one was *A Christmas Carol*, wrote by a man called Charles

Dickens. She'd read it to us every year on Christmas Eve. Course, she'd read it over and over to her own self the rest of the year, just to have somethin' to read. I don't think she even needed to get the book, 'cause she knew every word by heart. But she used it anyhow.

We all sat down around the fireplace and she began. "Marley was dead, to begin with. There was no doubt whatever about that. The register of his burial was signed by the clergyman, the clerk, the undertaker, and the chief mourner. Scrooge signed it."

We hung onto every word, listenin' to the story of Scrooge and how he found the goodness in Christmas and bein' nice to other people. Papa sat at the table, every bit as drawn in to the story as we were. So was Mama. She'd take breaks from cleanin' the turkey to listen.

Inez got to the part about all the ghosts that were

visitin' mean old Scrooge, and John got skeered, and, of course, so did Ruby. Frank spoke up and tried to calm 'em down. "You don't need to be skeered. This story happened in England. That's clear across the Atlantic Ocean. Everybody knows that ghosts can't cross water." That calmed down John, but not Ruby. I could tell 'cause she scrunched up so close to my left side that I thought she'd be on my right side any minute.

After a while, Inez got to the end of the story. "May that be truly said of all of us! And so, as Tiny Tim observed, God bless us, Every One! The end."

I looked to where Inez was sittin'. "That was a real nice story, Inez."

"Thanks, Roxie, but I didn't write it. I just read it."

"I know, but I bet that if that Mr. Dickens was to read it to us, it wouldn't be half as good."

Mama came out of her stall carrying one of John's stockins with her. "It's time for y'all to get into bed. But before you do, I need you to bring in one of your stockins and put it on the fire board."

I got up from the floor. "What for, Mama?"

"It's Christmas Eve. Don't you do the same thing every Christmas Eve?"

"Well, yeah, but I thought—"

"Stop thinkin' and do what your Mama tells you."

"Yes, Mama." We all ran to get our stockins and brought 'em back to put 'em on the fire board. Then Mama sent us up to bed.

After me and Ruby got up into the loft, I asked her, "Why do you reckon Mama wanted us to put out our stockins?"

"I don't know. You're the older one. You tell me."

"Papa's been gone an awful lot, but I know he couldn't have gotten into town, especially with all this snow."

"I don't know. You're the older one. You tell me."

"You don't know nothin' anyway, Ruby! I don't

know why I talk to you in the first place. From now on I'll go talk to the mules. What do you think about that?"

"I don't know. You're the older one. You tell me."

"Oh, just hush up and get in the bed." She did. "Not on my side!" I shouted. She huffed and scooted over.

After a bit, Mama climbed up the ladder. "I've gotta stay up for a while to finish cleanin' the turkey. I'm gonna tack up this old bedsheet so the light don't keep you awake." She nailed the sheet up to the rafters and started back down the ladder. "Night-night, Ruby."

"Night-night, Mama."

"Night-night, Roxie."

"Night-night, Mama." Then I turned to Ruby and whispered, "Night-night, skeerdy-cat." She let out one more huff and scooted away from me some more.

20 · *Christmas Mornin'*

I woke up to Ruby shakin' me.

"Wake up, Roxie! Wake up!"

"Leave me alone, Ruby. I ain't ready to get up yet!" I rolled over onto my side and covered my head with the quilt.

"But Roxie, it's Christmas!" Those words made me open my eyes, and I was out of bed as quick as lightnin'.

We raced to get dressed, and I was down the ladder in three steps. John was sittin' in Mama's rocker starin' up at the fire board. He turned his head when I leaped off the ladder. "I think Santa was here last night, Roxie."

Mama was at the stove. I rushed over to her. "Can we look in our stockins, Mama? Can we look in 'em now?"

"Not until everybody else gets out of bed."

Ruby ran in to wake Frank. I went into Inez and Frankie's stall. "Get up! Hurry!" I was pullin' 'em out of bed and throwin' their clothes at 'em.

Frankie was gettin' annoyed with me. "Stop it, Roxie. I'm gettin' dressed as fast as I can!"

I drug Frankie out of the stall and into the main room. Papa was at the table, with John sittin' on his knee. I asked Mama, "Can we look in our stockins now?"

"You can as soon as Frank brings in some firewood."

"Now, Mama? You want me to get some wood right now?"

"Frank Dockery, you've been pesterin' me for

three days to let you bring in the firewood."

"But Mama, the Christmas stockins!"

Papa slipped John down off of his knee. "Oh, Callie, let 'em have their stockins now. I'm afraid Baby John's gonna burst if we don't."

Mama chuckled a little bit and said, "Oh, Bass, I'm just havin' a little bit of fun with 'em. Go ahead, youngins, see what's in your stockins."

We grabbed our stockins off the fire board to see what was inside. It was candy. Not stick candy like we usually got, but molasses candy that Mama had made, wrapped in paper. Ten pieces each, and three cookies cut out in the shape of a star. John took the wrappin' off one of his candies and popped it into his mouth. Mama said, "Just eat one piece each for now. I don't want y'all to spoil your appetites. I'm makin' a big breakfast over here, and I expect it to be eaten."

Then I noticed somethin' under the Christmas tree. It was a big block with Mama's Sunday quilt coverin' it. That was the quilt Mama didn't use, except she'd put it on the bed when we had company. "What's that under the tree, Mama?"

"That's my Sunday quilt. You've seen it before."

"What's under the quilt?"

"You'll find out soon enough. Now, Frank, get me that firewood."

We ate our breakfast and washed up the dishes, all of us wonderin' what was under the tree. Then Papa called us over. "Everybody gather 'round the tree. I've got somethin' to show you." We all crowded in. "Y'all know I couldn't get into town, and I felt bad about that. So I thought I'd do somethin' about it." He pulled off the quilt and handed it to Mama.

Under the quilt was a big box made out of pine, with a lid that was hinged with two leather straps. The box had been stained red with pokeberry juice. Across the top in big black letters was written FRANKIE. "It's for you, Frankie. It's a hope chest.

Your Mama was just about your age when her Daddy made hers. You can start collectin' things to put in there, so you'll have housewares to get started with someday when you get married."

"Oh, Papa, it's beautiful," Frankie said as she stared wide-eyed at the hope chest.

Mama stood there holdin' the quilt, smilin' at Papa. Her eyes danced and sparkled, and they started to well up with tears. Papa looked at her. "The only reason I married your Mama was so I could get the things she'd collected in her hope chest. Well, the things in her hope chest and that sweet face of hers." That made Mama laugh, and she wiped her eyes.

Frankie reached out her hand and touched the top of the chest. She ran her fingers across her name. "Your printin' looks real nice, Papa."

She started to lift the lid, but Papa stopped her. "Now don't open it up just yet. There's more things inside it, for your brothers and your sisters."

John started jumpin' up and down. "Me first, Papa! Me first!"

"All right, Baby John, you'll be first."

Papa opened the chest and pulled out a stick pony. It was made from an old broom with a head cut out of wood. When John saw it, his eyes opened wide. Then he squinted. "Is that for me or Mama?"

Papa chuckled. "No, it's for you, Baby John."

John grabbed the pony and started gallopin' around the room, shoutin', "Getty-up! Getty-up!"

Papa went back to the trunk. "This is for Frank." He pulled out a checkerboard and a little sack filled with checkers. "I'll play you a game later on."

"Thank you, Papa."

Next there was a little shelf for Inez. It was about three feet long and had a carved back. It was stained with pokeberry juice, just like the chest.

"I'll hang this up for you, Inez. I thought it'd be

nice for you to keep your books and things on. So you can get 'em up off that dirt floor."

"It's perfect, Papa," Inez said.

Ruby was standin' beside me, tappin' her foot up and down with excitement. The tappin' was about to drive me crazy. "Papa, give Ruby her present next so she'll stop tappin' her foot."

"All right," Papa chuckled as he reached in the trunk. Ruby's present was a little bear cut out of wood, with arms and legs that moved. It was attached with string between two sticks. When the sticks were squeezed together, the bear would dance and turn flips. Ruby was delighted.

Then Mama said, "Don't forget, Bass, there's somethin' else in there for her."

He pulled out a doll. It was made out of corn shucks—its dress and all—except its hair was made out of corn silk. The doll was holdin' a little bunch of Mama's dried flowers. Inez looked at me, and we said at the same time, "Corn shucks!"

We started to laugh, and Mama looked at us. "What's so funny?"

Inez caught her breath. "Nothin', Mama. Just wait a minute. We've got something for you and Papa." She and Frankie ran into their stall and were back in just a few seconds.

"This is for you, Papa. It's from all of us." Frankie handed him a brown-paper package tied up with string. "Well, open it up!"

He undid the string and pulled out the brown shirt. "Well, now ain't that somethin'."

Mama looked at Frankie. "I said you could do some amazin' things with a needle and thread."

"Thank you, Mama."

Inez handed Mama a paper bag. "This one's for you."

She opened the bag. "Bass, would you look at this hat. Who made it?"

Ruby spoke up. "We all helped, but it was mostly Inez and Roxie. We made you another one, but the mule ate it."

"What?"

Inez laughed. "Nothin', Mama, it's a long story. We'll tell you about it later."

Then Papa opened the trunk and said, "As long as we're all gettin' presents, I reckon I'll give Callie one." He handed her another package wrapped in brown paper.

"Bass, what did you do?" she asked, smilin' as she opened it. It was the piece of glass that Papa had taken out of the window when he set up the stove. He had made a frame to go around it and had painted a picture on the back of the glass so that it showed through the front. It was a picture of a house with a little pine tree next to it.

"It's the house I'm gonna build you when the spring thaw comes. I'll plant you another pine tree, too, except this one won't be so close to the house."

Mama put the picture on the fire board and stood there lookin' at it for a minute. Then Papa walked over to her and put his hands on her shoulders. "I ain't got the whole thing planned out yet, but I can promise you that it'll be a heap bigger than the old house."

Mama reached up and patted Papa's hand. "That's a good thing, 'cause we're gonna be needin' more room."

Papa turned, walked away, and sat down in a chair. "Yeah, we've always needed more room. I figure I'll put the kitchen in the back so that you can—"

Mama turned around and interrupted him. "You didn't get what I was sayin', Bass. I was sayin' that we were gonna be needin' more room." Papa looked at her, and a funny look came across his face. Then he leaped up and let out a holler. He picked Mama up and twirled around and around.

Mama let out a laugh and said, "Put me down, Bass! You're liable to hurt the baby!"

John said, "He ain't gonna hurt me. I'm clear on the other side of the room."

"I don't mean you, Baby John. I'm talkin' about the new baby. You're gonna be gettin' a little brother or sister."

21 · *Quiltin' Scraps?*

We were so excited by the news that we all started talkin' at once. That is, all of us except for Papa. He just strutted around the room wearin' a big smile. I don't think you could've pried that smile off of his face with a crowbar.

Right away, Frankie started talkin' about gettin' cloth to make clothes for the baby. And there were a million questions. *Do you want it to be a boy or a girl? I wonder what it'll look like.* Then John climbed up into Mama's lap and asked, "When will the new baby get here?"

"Not until the summer, when the warm weather comes," Mama told him as she stroked his hair.

He looked puzzled. Then he concluded, "Oh, I get it! He can't get here till then on account of all the snow."

We all sat around tryin' to think up names for the baby, and we were talkin' up a storm. Then Mama said, "This is all well and fine, but I wish everybody would stop makin' such a fuss over me. It ain't like it's my first baby. Y'all seem to be forgettin' that it's Christmas. If I ain't mistaken, I believe that some-body still has a present comin'."

What with all the commotion, I'd completely forgotten. I started to get all tingly inside as Mama went over to Frankie's hope chest. The others had gotten such nice things. I couldn't imagine what might be in store for me. We all got quiet, waitin' to see what it was. Mama lifted the lid, pulled out my present, and handed it to me. "This is for you, Roxie."

My heart sank. It was the brown-paper package that Aunt Floss had sent. I took the box and said in a small voice, tryin' not to show my disappointment, "Thank you, Mama. I've been wantin' some quiltin' scraps."

A big lump tightened up in my throat, and I tried to hold back my tears. Mama started laughin'. Then she bent down close to me and brushed her hand against my cheek. "No, darlin', open it up and see what's inside."

I slowly pulled away the brown paper and lifted the box lid. There was crumpled newspaper inside. I pulled it out and looked at what was under it. The lump in my throat faded away as I stared down. It was a doll. A for-honest-and-goodness, store-bought doll. It looked up at me with its bright blue eyes. Its cheeks were pink and rosy, and blond curls surrounded its face. Mama spoke up. "There's another little dress in the bottom of the box. It's

the one that it had on when Aunt Floss sent it.
But I made the one it's got on now. I've been savin'
the scraps in my trunk for years. I thought you
might like it."

The dress was made out of the rest of my blue
print dress. There was a little lace around the cuffs
and collar, and a blue ribbon was tied around the
doll's waist.

"Do you like it?" Mama asked. "Do you, Roxie?"

The lump came back up into my throat, but I
managed to speak. "Yeah, Mama, I like it."

"Good, I thought you would. Now, be sure to
take real good care of it. And take special care of
the ribbon that's tied around its waist. It's the one
that I wore in my hair when me and your papa
got married."

"I know it is, Mama."

Then everybody started talkin' again—that is,
everybody except for me. I sat there holdin' my

doll, thinkin' about Aunt Floss and picturin' Mama sittin' in her rocker, sewin' the little dress. All at once we heard a sound comin' from outside. It was a ringin', jinglin' sound. Papa hushed us up. Then John said, "What's that?"

22 · *A Double Christmas*

rank opened the door and looked out. "It's Grandma and Grandpa!" We all rushed over to see, not believin' a word he was sayin'. But sure enough, he was tellin' the truth. They were comin' up the road in a sleigh pulled by two big brown horses.

Mama put her hand on her hip and said, "Well, goodness to heavens, I don't believe my eyes! Bass, you'd better run down to meet 'em before they see the house. It'll skeer Grandma to death."

Papa grabbed his coat and did like she said, wavin' his arms as he rushed down the hill. Mama turned to Frank. "Go help your Papa unhitch their horses. Frankie, you go help Grandma up the hill."

When they got inside the barn, there were hugs and kisses all around. Mama finally made us leave Grandma alone for a minute. "Now let her get inside. She's had a long trip." Mama sat her down in the rocker to warm by the fire. "I can't believe you made it all the way across the mountain in this snow. Where did you get the sleigh?"

Grandpa spoke up. "We borrowed it from Bert Woody." That was Papa's cousin. "Vic remembered that he had one sittin' in the field behind his house. It's a good thing he did. You know Vic. She was determined to get here one way or another. I was afraid she was gonna make me carry her the fifteen miles."

We told 'em all about the big tall pine tree and how we ended up movin' into the barn. Grandma listened as we each shouted out parts of the story.

She pulled John up onto her lap. "For goodness sakes, it's a wonder he wasn't killed!"

Grandpa laughed. "It'd take more than an old pine tree to kill this boy. He's a Dockery."

Mama sat down at the table. "I'm so glad you were able to get here, Vic. It just wouldn't have been Christmas without you and George."

"We wouldn't have missed bein' here for anything in the world," Grandma said as she hugged John close to her and kissed him on the top of his head. Then she looked up at Mama. "George knew that with all this snow, you and Bass wouldn't be able to get down to the store in Murphy to do your Christmas shoppin'. So he took that sleigh and went there himself."

Mama got to her feet. "George, you didn't!"

Grandpa George flashed a big smile and said, "Sure I did!"

Mama walked over to him. "Do you mean to tell

me that you went all the way down to Murphy, then all the way back up the mountain to get Vic, then traveled the fifteen miles to get here? It's a wonder you didn't kill yourself!"

John slipped off Grandma's lap and said, "It'd take a lot more than that to kill Grandpa. He's a Dockery!"

Grandpa picked up John and said, "You got that right, Baby John! You sure got that right!"

Grandma got her basket and gave each of us youngins a little paper sack. Inside each sack was an orange and two pieces of stick candy. It was like havin' a double Christmas. Then Grandpa smiled and handed Mama a little sack. "This is from that husband of yours."

Mama opened it and pulled out three handkerchiefs. They were light blue and had white lace around the edges. Mama winked at Grandpa and went over to Papa. "Why, thank you, Bass."

Papa put his hands in his pockets, looked down at the ground, and said, "Well, it wasn't exactly me that got 'em for you. I would've, if I'd had the chance, but what with all this snow, I just couldn't get down to—"

Mama stopped him from talkin' when she put her fingers under his chin and pulled his head up, so that he was lookin' at her. "I know you would've, Bass. That's why I'm sayin' thank you." They looked at each other for a long moment while the rest of us stayed real quiet.

Then John shouted out, "Grandma, Grandpa, let me show you the present I got!" He brought over his stick pony to show it off, and he kept insistin' that Grandma take it for a ride. Finally, she gave in. She sure was a sight with her dress hiked up above her knees, ridin' around the room on the stick pony. We laughed till it hurt.

Mama and Grandma started workin' on

Christmas dinner, while Papa and Grandpa took turns playin' checkers with Frank. We talked and gave each other the news. All about the baby that would be comin' in the summer and Aunt Floss and Uncle James. After a while, Ruby climbed up the ladder into the loft. A few minutes later, she called out, "Roxie, come up here for a minute."

"What do you want?"

"Just come up here for a minute."

I climbed up the ladder and made my way into the loft. "Yeah, what do you want, Ruby?"

"Here." She held out somethin' wrapped in a page from the Sears & Roebuck catalogue.

"What is it?"

"It's a present. I didn't get anything for the others, so I wanted to give it to you when we were alone. Well, are you gonna open it or not?" I pulled off the paper. It was a rock about the size of an egg. It was blue with little black specks, and it felt as smooth as glass. "I found it down by the creek last summer. I've been hidin' it ever since then, so I could give it to you for Christmas. I knew you'd like it 'cause it's blue."

"But I didn't get you nothin'."

"That don't matter. I didn't expect you to. But if you wanna get me somethin', just promise you won't kick me no more."

"OK, I promise." She leaned over and kissed me on the cheek. I didn't mind it this time.

23 · *Christmas Night*

We sat down to our big Christmas dinner. And big it was! Aside from the turkey, there was also each of our favorite vegetables. We all liked different things, so the table was loaded with green beans, squash, okra, sweet potatoes, and mashed potatoes, just to name a few. I was sure that the old door that Papa had turned into our dinner table would crash from the weight of all the food. But it didn't, 'cause the ten of us did a good job of takin' the weight off that homemade table.

Then we all sat around the fireplace listenin' to

Grandma and Grandpa tell stories about Christ-mases when they were little. They also told us Christmas stories about Papa, when he was as little as John. Those were fun stories, but none of us youngins could imagine Papa ever bein' as little as John. When our eyelids started droopin', Mama sent us off to bed and told us that there would be more stories in the mornin'.

Ruby and me climbed up into the loft, and I got ready for bed. I crawled under the quilt, clutchin' my doll. This time I got in on Ruby's side. She looked at me. "Hey, what are you doin'?"

"I'm gettin' into bed."

"But that's my side."

"I know, but I thought you might like to sleep on my side. I don't need the patch of blue print anymore. I've got my doll to keep me company."

She smiled and climbed under the covers, holdin' her doll, too. "Have you decided what you're gonna name your doll yet, Roxie?"

"No, not yet."

"Me neither." She laid there for a minute and then sat up. "I just thought of somethin'. What if one of us names our doll the same thing Mama names the new baby. Then everybody will get 'em confused."

"I wouldn't worry about that, Ruby. Whatever Mama names it, we'll probably just call it the baby, like we do Baby John."

She laid down, then sat up again. "Then what'll we call Baby John?"

"Just John, I reckon."

"That makes sense."

Mama came up into the loft and tucked the covers in around us. "Did you girls have a good Christmas?" We nodded yes.

"So did I," Mama replied.

Grandma's head popped up over the edge of the

loft. "Night-night, my pretty little Roxie."

"Night-night, Grandma."

"Night-night, my pretty little Ruby."

"Night-night, Grandma." Then she climbed back down the ladder. Mama kissed us both and climbed out of the loft.

After a minute, Ruby sat up. "I can't sleep on this side. It don't feel right. I ain't used to it. Let's switch back."

"All right." I crawled over her and she scooted under me. I laid my doll between us and reached for hers.

"What are you doin', Roxie?"

"I'm puttin' your doll here beside mine. I thought that they should lay side by side, 'cause they're sisters." She let go and I put her doll with mine. "Your doll sure is . . ." Then I stopped myself from talkin'.

Ruby asked, "My doll sure is what?"

"I was just gonna say that yours sure is pretty. In fact, I think she might be prettier than mine."

Ruby scrunched up close to me and said, "I don't know about that, Roxie. I reckon they're just about the same. It's like you said— they're sisters. Night-night, Roxie."

"Night-night, sister."

I could hear the grown-ups down below talkin' and laughin' into the night.

Papa was tellin' the story about Mama and the panther. I laid there thinkin' about what a wonderful day it had been. It seemed almost like a miracle. We'd thought that we weren't gonna have any Christmas at all, but it turned out to be the best one we'd ever had. As I listened to the grown-ups talk, I heard Papa say, "Then Callie said, 'While you're up there, 'my big strong man,' why don't you drag down that old panther I shot? I'd do it myself, but I'm just a helpless woman.'"

Grandma and Grandpa laughed out loud,
and so did Mama. But Papa laughed the loudest.
I closed my eyes, and I went to sleep.

Author's Note

In real life, Roxie Dockery is my mother. All of the characters in this book are drawn from real people in my family. Not everything in the book happened to them, but very well could have. Parents often had to be the doctors for their children, just as Papa was for Baby John. Children had to be "mountain smart," so they would know what to do when they had run-ins with panthers and other wild animals.

When Roxie was a girl, most mountain families didn't have the things that we take for granted today—things like cars, electricity, or even cameras.

The photos on the next pages were taken by tourists who asked to photograph my family and sometimes posed with them. They sent my family copies of the photos when they got back home.

Things have certainly changed since the 1930s, but if you visit the Appalachian Mountains today, you'll still find echoes from the past—people canning vegetables for winter, repairing and building their own homes, hunting and fishing, and doing all the other things they need to survive in such a remote, secluded place. Their resourcefulness and ingenuity still inspire me today.

Left to right: Mama, Papa, Baby John, Ruby, Roxie, Inez, Frankie, and Frank Dockery. Two tourists in foreground.

Roxy, Ruby, and Papa posing in an automobile.

Ruby at left, Roxie at right. Notice Roxie's shoes.
They weren't work boots—they were for every day.

Grandpa George and Grandma Vic, with their pig Betty!